Icecold Boss

Lana Stone

THE BILLIONAIRES OF NEW YORK 7

Copyright

Copyright © 2023 by Lana Stone
Loving Hearts Publishing LLC
2880W Oakland Park Blvd
Suite 225C
Oakland Park, FL 33311

Cover: Peter Bold
Lana on the net:
https://t.me/Lana_Stone_Liebesromane
www.instagram.com/lana.stone.autorin/

To become a test reader, for competitions, and for information about new releases, sign up now for my free newsletter, Lana's Favorites:

Dedication

As always, I dedicate this book to the love of my life.

And to all those who have the courage to face up to their past in order to fight for their future.

Blurb

He has what you need. You are what he wants...

What would you do if a hot billionaire made you an immoral offer?

Because student loans, paying rent, and her cat's latest vet bill aren't enough stress, a few more problems are added to Blossom's life.

Problem One: She falls into debt to Nolan Caldwell, the most successful man in town, because she accidentally scratches his car.

Problem Two: She is supposed to work for him to pay back the money, but he is an insufferable asshole.

Which brings us to another complication. Not only is Mr. Icecold a bastard, he's also handsome as hell, and arrogant to boot.

Which leads Blossom to her last, but perhaps, biggest problem.

Nolan Caldwell always gets what he wants.

And now he wants her.

Prologue

Hey, little pigeon. Welcome to Caldwell Tower.

If you're longing for rose petals that fall from a four-poster bed during cuddly sex, you've come to the wrong place, probably even the wrong world.

If you need trigger warnings, put the book down, you won't have any fun here.

But if you like the fact that I give good girls what they want, and bad girls what they deserve, stay and make yourself comfortable.

In front of me. On your knees.

Good girl.

Chapter One: Today, the Disasters are Sticking to the Soles of My Shoes.

Blossom

Slowly and deliberately, I maneuvered my lightweight Honda through the New York traffic, which had almost come to a standstill.

Today of all days, in addition to the normal rush hour traffic, there just had to be two detours due to construction, which clogged up the roads even more than usual and were preventing me from getting to my interview on time.

Just the thought of being late made my heart pound painfully against my ribs, because I really needed the job. The unexpected vet bill for my kitten's treatment had dealt a death blow to my bank account.

Think positive, Blossom! I urged myself.

I still had ten minutes, and Caldwell Tower was only two blocks away. I could already see the top of the building, surrounded by little white cotton candy clouds.

It was slow going, and it was getting very hot in my riding leathers; the start of summer had come pleasingly early this year. Luckily, the batteries on my alarm clock had died overnight, so I didn't have time for makeup this morning, so at least I didn't have to worry about runny mascara.

When it was clear that I would make no more progress on the road, I switched off the engine and maneuvered my bike to the curb to get some air. Without a headwind, I could hardly breathe under my helmet, and I could already feel heatstroke sizzling under the boiling sun.

I took off my helmet and shook out my blonde hair, which caused the bike to roll back a few feet. The next moment there was a bang, which sent my pulse racing to infinity.

This always happened when metal scraped against metal; I should realize that I wasn't back in my worst nightmares, but fear was never rational. Fear was my greatest enemy, which could not be suppressed with logical arguments or friendly pleas. On the contrary, the more rationally I wanted to act, the more clearly images flickered before my inner eye, images that I just wanted to forget.

My whole body tensed up. I just couldn't get rid of the memories that terrorized me almost every night.

Feeling electrified, I jumped off the bike and struggled to control my flight instinct.

A small but very loud part of me was going crazy as I tried to calm myself down, doing what I always did when the nightmares haunted me.

Streptopelia turtur. Columba livia. Streptopelia decaocto.

When someone tapped me on the shoulder, I jumped about a foot. Dark brown eyes caught my gaze. I had never seen eyes like those before. It was almost as if they could see into the abyss of my soul.

I was so surprised that my mind went totally blank. I had no idea why this man was continuing to stare at me so angrily.

Wow. My body relaxed visibly, and apart from the trembling of my right hand, which always took longer than the rest of my body, I slowly relaxed.

At the same time, Mr. Darkeye's glare made my heart jump further against my chest.

"What the hell was that about?" His voice was a harsh growl, and slowly I returned to noisy reality. He stared indignantly at my bike, which was in close contact with the driver's door of his car. A pretty fancy car, mind you.

"Thanks for asking, I'm fine," I replied, reflexively rubbing my trembling arm just to make sure I actually was okay.

"You owe me an answer." His facial expression made it clear that he wasn't used to repeating questions. Or having to collect debts. Still, it stung that he so clearly didn't give a damn about me.

He inhaled sharply. "Don't you have eyes in your head?" Again he pointed at my motorcycle, which was still leaning against his open door.

"Yes, I did, but I could ask you the same question. After all, you should have seen me," I replied, trying to defend myself. I don't know why, but he made me angry. Not just angry, but furious. Or was it something else that made my pulse shoot up again when he looked at me with those dark eyes?

"I saw you." The way he emphasized the words made my stomach tingle. "I just didn't foresee you suddenly rolling backward."

He was right; I had messed up; the accident was my fault. I had to face that fact whether I wanted to or not. And I certainly didn't want to, because my mountain of debt was now so high that I only had one option left, and I definitely didn't want to go back to Seattle.

"I'm sorry, it's been a difficult day," I mumbled. If I'd known how much chaos was lurking outside my front door, I wouldn't have gotten out of bed in the first place.

At least my right arm had finally stopped shaking. This guy already thought I'd lost my mind anyway, and the stress tremor in my hand certainly didn't make it any better, although I didn't think he'd even noticed. He was far too busy clenching his sharply chiseled jaw and giving me stormy looks.

"Give me your phone," he demanded without responding to my last statement, holding out his hand.

I blinked in surprise. "What?"

"Your cell phone. Now." His voice got all throaty, and he wore an expression that made it hard for me to disagree. Slowly, I got an inkling that he was as cold as he was beautiful.

I obeyed, and after he had entered his number into my contacts, he gave it back to me.

Nolan. At least I had a name to go with the face.

"I'm Blossom, by the way," I replied. It was only fair that he knew my name too.

"Instead of your name, I could use your insurance company's," Nolan replied coolly, sending a shiver down my spine.

It was only now that I realized that my Honda had not only bumped his car, but had left several long scratches.

Great, that was all I needed.

"Oh!" I gasped. I couldn't say anything else, because I felt dizzy. I did have insurance, but it was unlikely to cover the damage I'd caused, especially after I'd "accidentally" forgotten to pay the last few bills, since I'd needed to scrape together the money for Little Miss Scratchy's treatment.

"Oh?" Mr. McDreamy with a three-day beard raised a brow as he glared at me angrily. I didn't know if it was his handsome face, or the expression on it that made me melt and shudder at the same time. "Is that all you have to say?" He looked at me expectantly, almost as if I owed him an answer. But I didn't owe him anything, apart from the number of my expired insurance policy.

I pushed my Honda forward a little, to get a better look at the damage I had caused. My bike had survived the impact unscathed, but the paintwork on the car was scratched pretty deeply in some places.

"The scratches look bad, but it's only a tiny little problem," I said hoarsely, holding my thumb and forefinger together. Tiny was perhaps an understatement, but the main thing for me was that none of us had been hurt. I could compensate for a fender bender somehow, but not for anything bigger. Unfortunately, I had come to this realization the hard way.

I smiled awkwardly, trying to appeal to his humanity, but to no avail. His eyes darkened so much that they looked almost black, and I had to swallow hard. There was no question that he was of a different opinion.

"Do you have any idea what you're talking about?" he barked.

I admired the self-control he displayed, even though he was so angry. His tailored suit stretched taut across his broad shoulders, and his jaws ground against each other.

"I'll pay for the damage, okay?" I raised my hands placatingly, noticing as I did that my red nail polish was the same color as the paint on the sports car I had just scratched. "Or better still, I'll correct my mistake before the garage does the finishing work."

I grabbed the nail polish out of my backpack, remembering my best friend's words when she had leant me the color.

"So that you don't look like a wallflower at the job interview," she had told me, giving me a hug before I left today.

Her self-confidence was huge; she had no problem taking on even the biggest guys who would sometimes rough up the Royal Red, where we both worked. I loved working there, but the pay was so bad that I needed more than one job to keep my head above water.

"No, don't," Nolan ordered, growling, as I got down on my knees and liberally applied Ruby's nail polish to the scratches. At first it looked like I was really going to get away with it, but the next moment I realized that the substances in the nail polish were reacting with the car paint, just like in chemistry class when the teacher had mixed two chemicals that didn't like each other at all.

Whatever the damage had been before, I had just doubled or even tripled the cost, and given my insurance company another reason not to have to pay.

I watched in shock, my aggravation escalating more and more. Until Mr. Hot grabbed my wrist in a vice-like grip and turned me away from the car. In his hand, my wrist seemed tiny, and the intensity with which he held me made my breath catch.

He inhaled sharply as he stared at my hand. I resisted his grip, but nowhere near enough to signal that I really objected. It was more of a protest against my subconscious, which for some unknown reason found the touch exciting and tingling.

"I'm sorry," I whispered.

"It will probably take more than an apology and an innocent look."

God, this situation was killing me. I had no idea how to deal with the tingling sensation his hand left on my skin, or the trembling I felt when he looked down at me appraisingly.

I must still be in shock from the near-accident, otherwise I certainly wouldn't be thinking such thoughts. I stared at his big hand, noticing when his sleeve slid back a little that he was wearing a Rolex.

At first, I only noticed the time subconsciously, then I was struck by the realization that my job interview was taking place right at this moment.

I finally managed to break out of his spell and jumped back to my feet.

For a second, Mr. Sexy seemed to be just as upset as I was, but then his face hardened again.

"You're not just going to leave," he murmured as I swung back onto my Honda.

"Yes, I will. Because if I don't get to my interview now, you'll get your money in the form of returnable bottles, which you can pick up every week under the nearest bridge!"

He needed to know how serious I was. If I didn't get this job, Little Miss Scratchy and I would end up on the street, because my student loans were due at the end of the month, as well as the rent.

"Don't you dare leave me here!" he demanded in a throaty voice. My whole body shuddered at his command, but I had to do what would save my ass.

I pulled a business card from the Royal Red out of my jacket pocket and gave it to him.

"I work there, you can just ask Vince for my details. But please don't tell him about the accident," I begged.

"Royal Red?" He raised his left eyebrow questioningly. "Sounds like a strip joint."

Heat shot into my cheeks. "God no! It's a wine bar. I play the piano there." I put on my helmet. "I'll call you, Nolan, and I'll pay my debt. Somehow. Word of honor."

Then I flipped my visor down, started my bike, and weaved my way through the line of cars that had only moved a few feet since my accident, but now gave me enough room to get ahead.

When I arrived at Caldwell Tower, I parked my bike, stowed my leather gear, and trotted to reception, where a huge line of overworked secretaries was waiting. Hurray for the non-wrinkling shirts I always wore, otherwise my already late appearance would be even more chaotic. Despite this, my bad karma account seemed to have come due today; I must have paid it all back in one go, there was no other way to explain the events of this morning.

I wandered through the reception hall until I finally found a sign indicating the interview room. On the twentieth floor. And because fate really hated me today, the elevators were all occupied, which is why a second line snaked through the first floor and only ended at reception. But when I looked at the queue, there were also a few of my potential rivals waiting for the elevator.

"I am so going to regret this," I muttered to myself as I opened the door to the stairwell, intending to run away from the other contenders. Unfortunately, I wasn't one of those sports-are-my-life people, who ran on the treadmill all day. On the contrary, the only jogging pants I owned were used for lounging on the couch for weekend marathons with Ruby.

I trotted confidently up the first few floors, but with each step it became harder to catch my breath, and I slowed down.

After twelve floors my confidence was as good as dead, and the rest of me soon would be too if I didn't get a break. At least the pain distracted me from the throbbing I'd been feeling in my arm since the collision earlier.

To catch my breath, I leaned against the railing and pulled my phone out of my pocket. I needed emotional support.

Ruby picked up after the first ring. "Shouldn't you be at your job interview?" she asked, half-reprimanding, half-amused.

"Nice to hear you too," I replied, panting. "I had an accident."

"Are you all right?" Her voice immediately became serious. She didn't know every detail of my past, but I had touched on the most formative events here and there, even though I didn't like talking about them.

"Yes, all good." At least that was mostly the truth. When I took a look at the rest of the stairs I had to walk up, I felt quite different.

"You know you can be honest with me," Ruby admonished me in a motherly tone.

"It was just a little fender bender. I rolled backward into a car door," I tried to summarize what had happened.

"Phew, thank goodness!" She exhaled with relief. "And you're really all right?"

"Yeah." Luckily, Nolan's charisma had distracted me so much that I hadn't had the chance to completely panic. If our encounter had come about under different circumstances, I definitely wouldn't have just left him standing there. "Please don't tell Vince, you know how easily he gets worried."

"I won't tell him a word." Her voice was three octaves higher than normal, which was suspicious.

"Are you sure you can do it?" I asked. She was even worse at keeping secrets than I was.

"Yep, totally," Ruby replied hoarsely, and I knew immediately that she was going to fail.

"At least tell Vince not to worry. I'm doing really well. But let's get to the point," I went on to explain why I was calling her. I heard her exhale in relief, because I was no longer forcing her to keep a secret. "The short version of why I called—I'm late, the elevators are jammed, and now I'm rushing up the stairs to the twentieth floor."

"Way to go, Sporty Spice." Ruby let out a whistle through her teeth.

"As always, you're so not funny," I grumbled, and she began to giggle.

"Then what do you want to hear from me?" she asked innocently.

"A 'you can do anything you want, you just have to believe in yourself' would be great," I suggested.

"You can do anything you want, you just have to believe in it!" she parroted.

I couldn't hear Vince, who was working behind the bar with Ruby, but I knew he was giving her a questioning look. My friend wasn't really the believe-in-yourself-and-everything-will-go-well type, which was why speeches like that always sounded strange coming from her. Which is why I was all the more grateful to her for saying the words without her famous cynicism.

"Thank you, that's exactly what I needed." I stared up the stairs and started moving again.

"A little more self-confidence wouldn't do you any harm either. And speaking of which..."

"Speaking of what?" I gasped, my lungs heaving for air.

"Did you use my nail polish?"

"Yes, I did." I suppressed a sigh, because the stupid polish had tripled my problems without bringing the success Ruby wanted. Basically, the manicure had only made my day worse.

"You're wearing a super rare edition of Magic Red Velvet, Blossom! I want to hear more than a mumbled 'yes', sweetie. You are so going to rock that interview!"

Her confidence struck sparks, which were transmitted to me. I had to get this job, and the fact that I'd just walked twenty floors up proved how far I was willing to go. If I wore the nail polish half as proudly as Ruby would, I could only succeed.

"I can do it!" I replied. My voice didn't really sound convincing, but Ruby was satisfied with it.

"Very good. Get back to me when you get the job. I have to stop now, otherwise Vince will deduct the time for this interview from my salary. And with my pittance of a salary, that would mean I'd be working for free today."

I heard Vince protesting in the background, which made me giggle, then we hung up.

With renewed self-confidence, I entered the twentieth floor, misted myself with my emergency deodorant, and exhaled with relief when I saw that the door to the waiting area was still open, and interviewees were waiting.

But thinking that today was my lucky day was a big mistake. Before I even set foot over the threshold, I was confronted by a wiry guy whose sneering expression revealed that he was not an easy person to be around. He pushed his huge glasses back to the bridge of his nose and gave me a disparaging look.

"I'm supposed to be in there," I said, pointing past him to the group of women who were waiting on folding metal chairs for further instructions. I smoothed out my blouse and held up my application folder, which had been stowed in my backpack.

"You're too late," he replied tonelessly, making no secret of the fact that he didn't give a damn about me.

"It hasn't started yet," I replied, pointing to the waiting applicants in front of me.

"That doesn't matter. If you're late, you're out." He deliberately positioned himself in front of me so that I could no longer see into the room.

"What kind of stupid rule is that?" I cried out. Normally I was more careful with my choice of words, but could you blame me after today?

"The rule comes from the boss himself." Did I see a small, arrogant smile on his face, because I was conforming to all the prejudices and clichés that he had decided for me because of my unpunctuality?

I bit my lip to prevent another rude word from slipping out.

"I really need this job," I said, in agony, hoping to appeal to his humanity.

"I imagine the fifty applicants who showed up on time today do too." He smugly pushed his glasses back up the bridge of his nose once more as his gaze wandered around the room he was blocking for me.

The more of my competitors became aware of me, the more I wanted to sink into the ground. Even without my tardiness, it would have been hard enough to compete against these catalog beauties.

Caldwell Industries not only conducted one-on-one interviews, but also put its applicants through pretty much every endurance test the company had to offer, before making the final selection the next day. But as it turned out, the application round had gone ahead without me.

I didn't want to admit to myself that I had already lost, so I kept fighting, because I had reached the point where I had nothing left to lose.

"Please, I just want a chance to prove myself. I even put on Magic Red Velvet nail polish. It's super rare!" I had to be really desperate if nail polish was my last straw. Again.

The man's face softened and he beamed at me. "Well, if that's the case, it's a completely different matter. You are hired."

I blinked in surprise. "Really?"

"No," he said tonelessly, and his face immediately stiffened again. "Caldwell Industries doesn't give second chances. Now get out of here, or I'll call security." He gave me one last snide look, then slammed the door in my face.

"I'll leave my documents at reception in case you change your mind!" I called through the closed door before retreating with my head down.

I didn't want to conjure it up, but could today get any worse?

Yes. Because it seemed that all kinds of disasters were stuck to the soles of my shoes.

Chapter Two: The World Must Have Come Unhinged.

Nolan

When I entered my office, I was greeted by Dylan's smug grin. He didn't grin often, which made it seem all the more gloating.

"The world must be unhinged, if Nolan Caldwell is late for work." He made no secret of the fact that he was mocking my punctuality, but I didn't care. My rules had gotten me where I was today—at the top of the elite.

"I would have been on time, but..." I began, but he cut me off with a meaningful smirk.

"And then excuses too." He leaned against my desk, waving his hands in an exaggerated fashion.

"Not now," I growled. I sat down at my desk to switch on the hands-free system that connected me to my assistant. "Karen!"

Silence. Then Dylan cleared his throat.

"She works for me now, remember, but you can have her back. I have my own assistants," he said in a diplomatic tone; it was no secret that he liked Karen even less than I did.

It was only now that I remembered that the post of my personal assistant was vacant today, because the interviews had not yet been completed. But I'd rather have no assistant than Karen.

I pierced Dylan with a serious look until his grin disappeared and I could continue talking.

"No, she's staying with you. She's signed all the confidentiality agreements, and knows the key details of our project almost as well as I do." I remained deliberately calm, knowing that I was difficult in this respect. I never trusted anyone's word, so I drew up contracts for everything.

"If you say so. And you're sure there was no other reason to get rid of her?" He gave me a knowing look and I knew the question was rhetorical.

"Don't be ridiculous," I said, averting my eyes. He had hit the bull's eye, but I wasn't ready to admit it. A few more days and he would know exactly why I wanted to get rid of my former assistant so quickly.

"I never make a fool of myself," he replied, striking a completely ridiculous pose. Then he ran to the door and beckoned Karen in, who had been waiting outside.

"Yes, sir?" She didn't give Dylan a glance, but licked her lips and looked at me expectantly. There was no question that he knew why she was now working for him instead of me.

"I need an appointment for the garage. And someone has to take care of the insurance stuff." Just thinking about the damage to the paintwork made my blood start to boil.

"For the Maserati? What should I report to the insurance company?" asked Karen, leaning forward so far that her scantily covered breasts almost jumped out at me.

"The varnish has taken a beating," I growled. My hands clenched into fists as I thought about how the nail polish had further ruined the $100k custom paint job. But what actually made me furious was the look on the girl's face after I grabbed her wrist.

Had I ever seen such big, innocent eyes? And had eyes ever triggered this strange feeling in me? No. All I knew was that I wanted to throw up; I wasn't usually the sentimental type.

"Ouch," said Dylan, because he knew how much the car meant to me. "Heads are going to roll. Or have they already rolled? They'll probably roll all the way to California."

"It remains to be seen whether heads will roll," I said thoughtfully, turning up the volume on my phone so as not to miss any calls. This earned me another skeptical look from my best friend. Then I handed Karen the Royal Red business card so that she could sort out the insurance issues.

"Speak your mind, or stop looking at me like I've lost mine," I demanded to Dylan, who kept staring at me like I was a puzzle he was determined to solve.

He raised his arms placatingly. "It's all right, I didn't say anything."

I looked at Karen, who was still standing in the doorway, listening to our conversation.

"Do you need an extra invitation? Dylan won't be here all day, so hurry up."

"Of course, sir." She gave me a lascivious look that made me nauseous. I didn't like brunettes. And I certainly didn't like cheap hookups. In retrospect, I couldn't figure out why I'd stuck my cock in her mouth after the last project. It had been insignificant. So insignificant, in fact, that I hadn't drawn up a contract beforehand. And by God, I used contracts for everything.

She left the office, but before she closed the door I stopped her once more.

"And bring me a coffee from Daisy's, I haven't had any today." I usually drank a double espresso from the cafe every morning, which was so strong that it could bring the dead back to life. That was the only reason I'd parked the Maserati there, instead of in the underground garage of Caldwell Tower.

"Of course," she said, closing the door behind her.

"Where's Bruce?" I asked when we were alone. My left side immediately stung, because he had landed a lucky shot there during our last training session and it still hurt.

"How should I know?" Dylan asked with a shrug. He had taken quite a beating last time too, but didn't let the pain show. When it came to kickboxing, the three of us didn't know our limits, or at least interpreted them very generally. We were incorrigible in that respect, even after all these years under Donnie's good influence.

"When it comes to the merger, he should be here," I replied. We were currently working on combining three of our subsidiaries, in order to increase the capital fivefold within a year.

"You and your love of rules." Dylan crossed his arms in front of his chest and rolled his eyes.

"Where would we end up if we lived in a world without rules?" I looked at him seriously, expecting an honest answer. I had learned the hard way that a world without rules was a lost world. If you had no principles, you would betray everything and everyone at some point.

"We wouldn't get anywhere, but that doesn't mean you need sets of rules and contracts for *everything*," he countered with a sigh. He threw himself down on the black leather chair in front of my desk and looked at me calmly, waiting for an answer.

"I have my reasons," I growled without going into detail. *Speaking of the devil,* I reminded myself to follow my morning routine.

I opened the bottom drawer, took out a bottle of bourbon, and poured myself a glass. Even after so many years, the taste was still repulsive, but I finished it and put the bottle and glass back in the drawer.

Dylan had stopped asking years ago why I drank bourbon every morning, even though I disliked the taste, because I never talked about it. There were also things he never talked about. And Bruce probably had the most secrets of any of us.

"Shall we, then?" I asked, spreading my arms.

"In a minute. Let's instead talk about how someone scratched the only thing you've ever shown emotion toward, and it leaves you cold." He leaned back and looked at me smugly. As if he knew what was going on in my head.

We were friends, but he didn't have a clue. To be honest, I didn't know what to make of it myself. The way she had looked at me was driving me crazy. Once I'd clasped her petite wrist, I simply couldn't let it go. What's more, I hadn't been able to take my eyes off her full lips.

I had been angry, no question about it. Furious in fact, because Dylan was right, my car meant everything to me. It was the first thing I'd bought with my hard-earned money. The car was proof that I had broken out of the vicious cycle my family had banished me to.

"Would you believe me if I said I didn't know?" I asked, more to myself than to Dylan.

"No." He shrugged. "You always get to the heart of things. You're the definition of getting to the heart of things. And you're the definition of rule-loving. And your number one rule is to always get to the heart of things. So? What went down earlier?"

"Normally, the rules are clearer," I replied thoughtfully. But when eyes as green as emeralds got involved, it clouded my view of the big picture.

"But not for paint scratches?" Dylan furrowed his brows questioningly.

"She'll pay for the damage. Somehow. And that's the end of the matter for me." I didn't want to talk about this situation any longer, because I wasn't used to not being able to assess things clearly. And for a woman to upset me like that and then just leave me standing there... It was an unprecedented situation for me.

"You? So it's about a woman." He looked at me meaningfully, but I just grimaced.

"Now you're just making a fool of yourself." I waved him off and pulled a pile of files out of the top drawer of my desk, which I pushed toward him. "Sign this."

"More contracts? I'd love to, buddy. It's not like we've known each other forever."

It was no exaggeration. Dylan, Bruce, and I had known each other for half our lives. We had met at the most difficult time of our lives, and if I didn't know better I would say that our fights had saved our asses.

Donnie, our old coach, always claimed it was the team spirit ,and he was probably right, but sometimes I also thought that kicking each other's heads once in a while helped to clear our minds.

"Tell me about the girl," he demanded after signing the papers, putting his head to one side thoughtfully. "Or wait, you'd better tell me why all the women keep eye-fucking you. Is it because of your gloomy 'I'm-so-male-and-silent' aura?" He was deliberately teasing me with this question, because at least as many women eye-fucked him on a daily basis.

"You tell me, Mr. I'm-So-Silent," I countered with a grin, knowing it would drive him up the wall.

"We both know that your deep waters are pretty calm, whereas mine are always bubbling under the surface." Dylan was temperamental, it was true, but I'd never seen him lose control.

"From the outside, it makes no difference," I replied coolly.

"Possibly." He nodded thoughtfully. "Then at least tell me how I can get rid of the women who keep talking my ear off about how great you are." He exhaled heavily and pulled his phone out of his pocket without really looking at the screen.

"Jealous?" I kept grinning because Karen was the biggest trigger for all of us at the moment.

"Fuck no. I'm enjoying my peace and quiet. The one you destroyed, by the way," Dylan replied, annoyed.

"As hard as it is for me to say it out loud, you need Karen. At least until the merger is over, otherwise I would have fired her long ago." Admittedly, it wasn't that simple. In my contract mania, I had drawn up watertight agreements. So watertight, unfortunately, that it had taken me a long time to discover a loophole that would allow me to get rid of Karen.

"And how do I get rid of her then? When she realizes that she won't end up with you, Miss Opportunism will try me. So, what do we do about her?" He stuffed his phone back into his pocket.

"Find a crucifix and an exorcist?" I replied dryly.

Dylan stood up, shaking his head, and walked to the window to let his gaze wander over the skyline. "You're being particularly unfunny again today." His voice was toneless, and his look signaled that he was about to take a swing at me. It wouldn't have been the first fight in my office, and certainly not the last.

"Thank you." I smiled appreciatively. "You could pass it on to Bruce."

He turned to me and leaned against my desk, the way he always did when he was thinking about something without admitting that he was thinking about it.

"That would be a pretty bad move," he muttered, but I could see from his face that he didn't think my idea was bad at all. He was arguing with himself, so I fired back.

"We also fight below the belt," I pointed out. Ironically, I insisted that there were no rules in the ring. It was the one place where I didn't have to think about anything. There was only anarchy and brute force, which was somehow relaxing for my mind.

"True again," Dylan agreed with a shrug.

"Let's go to Left Hook today," I suggested indifferently, trying not to let on that I was in desperate need of a sparring session.

"Okay. The loser gets Karen." Dylan held out his hand to me, which I refused.

"After. The. Merger," I growled.

He immediately raised both hands in surrender. "Okay, okay. Get back down off your high horse; or rather, get back in your scratched Maserati."

"Do you want to take a beating right here?" I scowled at him from a seated position, because I didn't need to get up to meet him at eye level.

"You could try," he replied with a grin and half-heartedly raised his hands upward to cover himself.

I was almost inclined to really take a swing at him, but I had rules I needed to abide by. I lived by a code that I'd never broken, and even Dylan's provocations, tempting as they were, couldn't entice me to break them.

"Let's get to work." I shoved him the next stack of files we had to go through. The sooner we started working, the sooner I could get out of the office and back to Left Hook Haven, to take my mind off the war raging in my head.

Chapter Three: A Charming Synonym for Uncharming Things.

Blossom

As my fingers glided over the keys of the piano, the world around me regained its balance. What's more, my problems simply disappeared as if they had never existed.

Poof. Gone.

It became all the more difficult for me to stop playing again, because I knew that the problems around me would rematerialize. In fact, the chaos was so great that I couldn't entirely clear my head even while playing. And the pain in my arm reminded me why I would never make it to the big leagues as a pianist.

If it were up to me, I would play much more often at the Royal Red, but inflation had hit here too. If I wasn't something like a daughter to Vince, he would have replaced me long ago with a Spotify playlist, and the guests would probably still be happy.

Sighing, I finished the last song before taking my break and heading to the bar. It was only late afternoon, but the place was still fully booked. The Royal Red was a hidden secret for anyone who liked classical music and good wine, no matter what time of day.

"Give me the full blast," I said to Ruby, who was standing behind the bar waiting for my order.

"A Coke, with extra caffeine, coming right up," she replied with a grin. She grabbed a tall glass and filled it up.

"And throw a shot in there," I added.

She frowned and looked at me questioningly. "Sure?" She glanced sideways at Vince, who acted unconcerned, although he was watching us with eagle eyes. She shrugged. "Uh, yeah. Sure."

Normally, I didn't drink when I had to play. But normally my existential fears only nibbled gently on my little toe; today they were biting into my leg like a Rottweiler.

"Coming right up." She poured a shot of rum into the glass, pushed it across the bar to me, then she patted my hand and gave me an encouraging look. "It's on the house."

I hadn't told anyone about my botched interview, but they both knew how the day must have gone because of my silence.

"I'll be poor if you give away all the drinks, Ruby." There was a note of rebuke in Vince's voice, but she just rolled her eyes.

"It's Blossom we're talking about here. Am I supposed to charge her for the drink?" she countered in a pointed tone.

"Not you," he replied and winked at me. "But the other young ladies and gentlemen to whom you slide cocktails across the bar with meaningful looks."

"I'm just keeping all my options open," she replied with a grin. That was typical Ruby. Quick-witted, cheeky, and absolutely adorable.

"Flirt with whoever you want, but I'll deduct the next free drinks from your wages." He crossed his arms in front of his chest and looked at her with a fatherly gaze.

"You don't let me have any fun." She snorted playfully, but didn't disagree. "Speaking of which, how's your fun going, Blossom? When was the last time you treated yourself to a hot guy to take your mind off everyday life?"

Heat shot into my cheeks and I gasped for air. I found it hard to hide my indignation because Ruby kept teasing me about my virginity.

"Believe me, relationship drama is the last thing I need right now," I replied, hoping that she would change the topic. But my best friend didn't give up that easily.

"I'm not talking about your persistent search for Mr. Right, just Mr. Right-For-A-Night." She grabbed her bottle of beer and toasted me.

"We've already been over this." I sighed and looked helpfully at Vince, who put down the glass he had been polishing and threw the towel over his shoulder. He wanted to say something, but someone tapped me on the shoulder from behind.

"You played fabulously," said a young man in a suit.

"Thanks, I'll get right back to playing," I replied, staring at my drink. I often got compliments on my music, especially on the songs I composed myself, and every single bit of adulation was like a punch in the face. Sometimes the compliments weren't compliments at all, but just indirect requests to keep playing.

"You should be playing on the big stages of this world, not in such a dingy hole in the wall," the guy continued behind me.

"Hey!" growled Vince.

The guy raised his hands in a placating gesture. "Sorry, I didn't mean it like that."

"Thank you. But I feel very comfortable here." I smiled awkwardly at the guy and pulled the long sleeve of my red dress over my wrist.

To numb the burgeoning pain I took a big gulp, because as much as I wished for it, I would never achieve the career as a pianist that I had worked hard for my whole life, and that I had taken on the horrendous college debt to try to achieve.

When the man finally disappeared, Ruby looked at me, shaking her head.

"Are you proud of yourself?" she asked cynically, looking after the guy who had unknowingly poured more salt into my open, gaping wound.

"Why should I be proud of myself?" I asked, confused.

"Because you turned down an incredibly hot guy who was obviously interested in you?" She shrugged and gave him an eyebrow lift that some men would kill for.

"He was just praising my music," I said, shrugging because I didn't understand her drama. "That often happens when I play."

"Yep. And every single time, it's a charming synonym for 'I want to fuck you'," she said, without missing a beat. She was much more open and direct about such things than I would have liked.

"Ruby!" I almost jumped up from my bar stool. "Your charming synonyms for uncharming things are highly inappropriate."

"It is what it is, sweetie. Deal with it." She grinned at me unabashedly.

"You're impossible." I sighed heavily and looked over both shoulders, afraid that someone might overhear our conversation. But no one was interested in us, everyone was busy with their own things.

"And that's why you love me so much. Someone has to tell you the truth sometimes."

"Yes, you're an expert at smashing every truth in my face like a sack of bricks," I replied tonelessly.

"Thank you." She beamed at me.

"That wasn't a compliment!" I continued to protest, but it just bounced off her.

"Oh yes it was." She winked at me, but Vince put a hand on her shoulder to slow her down.

"You've embarrassed her enough, time to chill." His fatherly tone warmed my heart. I missed my family, but I hadn't been able to stay in Seattle for a single day after my accident. And because they hadn't wanted to give up their jobs and their lives there, I had moved to New York alone to build a new life and a new family.

"Thanks, Vince," I said.

"Yeah, thanks, Vince," Ruby grumbled sarcastically. "Sacks of bricks are overrated."

"Speaking of painful truths..." he paused, as if thinking about how he should ask his next question.

"How did your interview go?" he finally said. I snorted and threw my head back, fighting the tears that were burning behind my eyelids.

"That good?" he asked, knowing the answer already. But he was right, if I didn't talk about it, I would only keep it bottled up, and that was just as unhealthy as throwing alcohol on the problem.

"It went terribly, and I can rule out having a job there," I said, trying to keep calm. Just the thought that I would soon be on the street gave my heart a twinge. "And my next paycheck will probably go toward fixing the car I scratched today."

"I'm glad you brought that up..." When Vince looked at me like that, it couldn't mean anything good. I held my breath until he continued. "I'm afraid it's more likely to be your annual salary. For the next few years," he muttered.

I gasped in shock. "How much can a coat of paint possibly cost?" I asked. I had expected a few hundred dollars, but judging by the look on his face, we must be in a different price range.

"According to his secretary, who wanted your details for the insurance, fifty thousand dollars. Maybe more, because the paint is now only produced and used in Europe."

I felt dizzy.

"Fifty thousand dollars." I let the sum melt in my mouth and began to hyperventilate. "Where am I going to get that kind of money?"

My whole body trembled with fear.

"You could stay with me until you get back on your feet," Ruby suggested with a smile.

"You and your sister barely have any room in your one-bedroom apartment as it is; I don't want to get on your nerves." I took the second drink that Vince shoved at me pitifully and gulped it desperately.

"You and Little Miss Scratchy are family," she replied firmly.

"Thank you." I squeezed her hand, grateful for her support, but we both knew I could never accept her offer. She had enough problems of her own, and too little space. Another solution had to be found, and quickly.

"So what do you want to do now?" Vince gave me a look that made my heart tighten. I knew he would help me if he could, and that his heart was bleeding because he couldn't.

I pulled my phone out of my purse. "I'm going to call Nolan and beg him to give me an extension, because my insurance won't pay."

"Why won't the insurance company pay? Shouldn't you at least try? Why have insurance, if not for cases like this?" Ruby looked at me indignantly, because it wasn't usually my style to give up before the fight had begun. But to be honest, I was dog-tired.

"I can save myself the trouble. I caused the accident myself. And I've recently... misplaced the bills for my insurance," I explained.

"Oh, sweetie." She put on a pitying face and patted my hand awkwardly.

"What? I had a choice between a stupid insurance policy and urgent treatment for my cat. I didn't even think about what has priority," I said defensively.

"Okay. Then I'd at least advise you to make a video call if you're going to beg him, literally, on your knees not to sue you into the ground."

"You're optimistic," I muttered dejectedly.

"If you bat your endlessly long eyelashes at him, which I'm not a bit envious of by the way, he'll fall for you for sure!" She gave me an exaggerated demonstration of what she meant by that.

I faltered, because Nolan's words back at the crash site immediately resonated with me.

It's going to take more than your big, innocent eyes.

Unconsciously, I grabbed the wrist he had gripped. Compared to his hands and the rest of his body, I had seemed dainty, almost fragile, and I had liked it in a way that made me shudder.

"You're not making it any easier for me." Still, I was glad for her attempt to lighten the mood.

Ruby was the exact opposite of me. Confident, strong, and aware of her charms. I, on the other hand, was happy to stay in the shadows, or hide behind a large grand piano.

I held up my phone, and Vince immediately pointed to his anti-phone sign. He always enforced this rule mercilessly, which I usually loved him for, but not just then.

"I get it, I'll go to the back. And if it doesn't work out, I'll just sell a kidney, I've got two of them." I slid off the bar stool, finished my glass, and knocked on the table with my fist.

"Do you even know where you could sell kidneys for a profit?" Ruby asked with a raised eyebrow.

"I'll just try the phone book under 'B', for black market," I replied with a shrug.

"I didn't know you could be cynical," Ruby said with a proud grin.

"That wasn't cynicism. It was my dying optimism, whimpering quietly to itself and hoping that it will soon be over," I replied soberly.

"Hope dies last," she replied. I was taken aback by her perceptiveness, but then she took a breath. "That's the stupid thing about it. It dies last. You cling on to something that will never happen, when you would probably have given up much quicker without hope, so that you can look forward. And at some point, hope dies anyway. Whichever way you look at it, maybe you should give your hope a mercy kill and go in a different direction."

"Please promise me you'll never try to cheer me up again. You're really bad at it," I said half-seriously. Ruby just couldn't get out of her skin, but I gave her credit for trying to comfort me anyway.

"I promise."

Then, muttering a prayer to anyone who might be listening, I made my way to the storeroom, intending to beg Nolan tooth and nail to grant me a reprieve.

Chapter Four: Since When Do You Insist on Rules?

Nolan

I raised my fists protectively in front of my face. Only now I was finally able to let down the rest of my guard.

At Left Hook Haven, a fighter left the outside problems outside, and focused on the fight. That was the only rule Donnie had ever made, and he still enforced it.

I was in the ring with Bruce, while Dylan had nonsensically declared himself the referee, even though I always insisted on a fight without rules. Outside, rules were my sacred creed, but here it was just my skills and a burning anger that I had to get rid of somehow. I trusted my skills and my intuition. I was a born kickboxer, even if you couldn't tell when I was wearing my tailored suits.

"Ready?" asked Bruce at the other end of the ring. He bounced lightly on his feet from left to right and waited for my confirmation.

"I've practically already won," I replied calmly.

"Dream on, buddy." He shook his head, then raised his hands upward in a fighting stance.

I grinned. "How many times have I won against you?"

"You've lost at least as many times," he countered, glancing conspicuously at the large bruise on my flank. I didn't put any stock in it, but when I got bruises or bruises, I wore them with pride; to me it was a sign of discipline that I fought despite the pain and never gave up.

"Touché," I replied, then I gave the signal. The fight began, and we gave each other nothing. We were best friends, but that only worked because we didn't show any consideration for each other in the ring. I needed exactly that to relax, and the other two had their own reasons for always going to the limit.

"Where's your fancy car anyway?" Bruce asked, trying to provoke me after we had exchanged a few blows. He knew how important my car was to me, which is why he deserved the kick in the side that he didn't see coming.

"You know exactly where the car is," I growled. In no possible world could Dylan keep the accident to himself.

"Maybe I just wanted to rub salt in the wound," he teased with a grin.

"Salt that you got from who, exactly?" I looked reproachfully at Dylan, who was leaning on the ring ropes and watching our fight with eagle eyes so that he would have an advantage against the tired winner later.

"But maybe you want to lose without admitting it?" Bruce asked. His fist flew toward me, which is why he got my full attention again.

"I'd better ask you that, since you've been provoking me all this time." Such jibes between us were normal; we all felt that it strengthened the friendship between us even more when there was no belt to fall below inside the ring.

"It's when you get angry that the fight gets interesting." Bruce kicked left, feinted, and then switched to the right leg, which I blocked at the last moment. "So, who's the girl who's been at your mercy? Your future wife?"

I suppressed the reflex to curse, but instead I punched him so hard in the face that he screamed and clutched his forehead as blood began dripping from it.

"You scream like a girl," I said dryly.

"Fuck you, dude!" His eyes blazed with anger, directed not at me but at himself, because he should have anticipated the blow. But after a second, the anger faded and a grin appeared on his face, because my punch had been damn well placed.

I half-heartedly went for the next blow, but then dropped my hands again; Bruce had to tend to his laceration before I could continue. Maybe he had taken enough today.

"Lucky shot," he muttered before getting out of the ring to put ice on his forehead. Donnie always put a bucket of it next to the ring as soon as we entered Left Hook Haven.

"It's your own fault if you tease him about the chick he doesn't want to talk about," said Dylan with a grin, just as teasingly as Bruce.

"Do you want to bleed too?" I asked cynically, tightening the bandages around my hands. My knuckles were throbbing after the last blow, but I hadn't reached my limit yet. I wasn't going to stop before then.

"You could try," Dylan replied, accepting my challenge.

"Don't be too hard on him, buddy. Dylan's got nothing but his beautiful face," Bruce interjected, which made me grin.

"Funny," Dylan said tonelessly, then climbed into the ring to fight me.

"No talking about my car or the woman who wrecked it," I growled, because I was getting impatient. I wasn't here to chat, I was here to get rid of the damn thoughts that were haunting me today.

"Since when do you put down rules in the ring?" he asked with his eyebrows raised.

"Since you're breaking the only rule we have here," I replied, sighing with annoyance.

"Shit, our emotional baggage is outside." Dylan looked at me, confused. "Unless you want to say the accident is getting to you."

"Or the girl," Bruce added. They both caught hard looks from me.

"Imagination, boys. We're here to fight, so let's fight." I said, shutting them down. Not because I didn't want to say anything to them, but because I couldn't. I trusted them blindly, they were the only people I had ever been able to rely on.

But that didn't apply to my feelings, which were mostly irrational and even more painful.

"Ready?" I asked, and Dylan nodded.

The fight began. He had much better cover than Bruce, but I still landed a few hits. At the same time, I also had to take a few hits. I wasn't masochistic, but I would have been lying if I said I didn't enjoy the fight to distract me from the chaos inside me.

I remained silent, but my face darkened more and more until Dylan raised his hands in appeasement, asking for a quick break.

"It's okay, it's okay, you don't want to talk about it, I get it."

"There's nothing to talk about," I grumbled. "Let's get on with it already." I picked up my guard and shifted my weight to get ready to fight again.

"You got it," Dylan replied, checking his bandages one last time. Then we got started again.

He didn't make it as easy for me as Bruce, but I still had the upper hand. No wonder, after all the shit that had been going through my head today. Again and again, I pushed him into the corner and landed direct hits, but I also took them well. When he kicked me in the flank, right on the bruise, my breathing stopped for a second and I let my guard down. He used this to fire a volley of punches at my upper body until I was able to pull my hands back up and strike back.

After a long battle and endless strikes on both sides, we agreed on a draw.

We sat down at the edge of the ring and drank water. In the meantime, Bruce had been treated by Donnie and was almost as good as new.

"How is the merger of our subsidiaries progressing?" he asked, sitting down next to us. It was a rhetorical question, because although he was taking over a third of the new company, he wasn't interested in the business side of things. He was the exact opposite of Dylan and me when it came to business.

Nevertheless, we felt compelled to answer him.

"Good," I replied. At the same time, Dylan let out an annoyed sigh and struggled not to spit out the water he was drinking onto the floor.

"Could you two be any more contradictory?" Bruce asked, looking at us in turn.

"It's going well. I don't know what's wrong with him," I replied with a shrug. I really didn't know why he was so annoyed when I asked about our merger. Until this morning, I had thought that everything was going according to plan.

"I have to deal with the problems you're responsible for," Dylan explained. He tapped his index finger against my chest and grimaced.

"And what problems would that be?" I had no idea what he was talking about.

"Your commitment issues, what else?"

"Because you're so compatible with relationships," I countered matter-of-factly, because neither of us was eager for a relationship and neither of us could deny it.

"What does emotional instability in your personal relationships have to do with the merger?" Bruce deliberately excluded himself, although he was probably the one of us who talked the most about his one-night stands.

"I'd like to know that too," I said, looking at Dylan expectantly. "Enlighten us, please."

"One word is enough to explain everything," he said, tapping his chin with an outstretched index finger.

"Oh yeah? Now I'm curious." Bruce threw away his lukewarm ice pack and replaced it with a new one without even making a face.

"Karen," Dylan said simply, once he was sure he had our full attention.

"Ugh. Do we have to talk about her again?" I pressed the bridge of my nose between my thumb and forefinger and suppressed a groan.

"Yes. Again. Do you have any idea how exhausting it is that every five minutes she's looking for a reason to bring you something, or to work for you again?"

"Give her a few more days until she runs after the next rich jerk," I replied. Karen wasn't bad-looking, but I'd rarely seen an uglier character. In the time she had worked for me, she hadn't missed a single chance to flirt with me, or any other potentially rich man. And yet she of all people should have learned that billionaires don't settle for cheap.

"Ten bucks says Dylan's the next rich sucker," Bruce said with a grin.

"Ten dollars? You're one of the richest men on the East Coast, damn it! A bet like that is almost embarrassing." Dylan took off his shirt and wiped the sweat from his forehead.

"Money is money. Besides, we all know that the bet isn't about the money, it's about your tarnished pride," Bruce fired back.

"Ten dollars that Dylan isn't rich enough for her," I joined in. I didn't specify what exactly I meant by "rich", because when you've reached a certain point, as we had, money no longer plays a role.

"Fuck you both. I'll bet my Porsche you're both wrong." Dylan pointed to the keys to his car, which were lying on the small table next to our phones and other belongings. I noticed the flashing display of my phone, which was on silent.

"Excuse me a moment," I said. I got up to take the call, which was from a number I didn't recognize. Only a handful of people had my number, and they were all stored in the phone's contacts, which is why this call piqued my interest.

"Yes?" I answered.

"Nolan?" Her voice sounded different through the static of the phone, but I recognized her immediately.

It was her. The woman who'd scratched my holy grail and who, for reasons I didn't understand, I didn't resent as much as I should.

"Yes." That was all I said as I moved further away from Bruce and Dylan.

"This is Blossom." Her voice trembled unsteadily and in my mind's eye I saw her wide eyes.

"I know," I replied calmly, waiting for her to tell me the reason for her call. According to Karen, the insurance company had already started to sort it out.

"I promised I'd pay back the debt, and I will, but I can't do it now." She sighed heavily.

I'd dealt with investors often enough to know that I wouldn't see any money when sentences like that came out.

"Why?" I asked in a demanding tone, because I hated having to ask. Normally, I was used to things being put in a nutshell.

"There are two big reasons," she began to explain. "First, because your insurance company is demanding an outrageously high sum that I will have to work for forever."

She paused to collect herself.

"And second?" I asked, because patience was not my strong point in this respect.

"I didn't get the job as an assistant." Her words were quiet and mumbled.

"Were you not qualified enough?" The question slipped out as the businessman in me came through and immediately analyzed the situation.

"What? No," she stammered, before regaining her composure. "I'm qualified."

"Where did you even apply?" I continued to ask. Within a radius of two blocks, I'd blocked out all the big companies.

"Caldwell Industries," her reply came just as hastily as the first.

I faltered when she mentioned the name of my company.

"Be on the executive floor in half an hour," I growled, without thinking any longer about my crazy idea.

"But I'm working right now," she protested hesitantly. "My second job. I can't make ends meet with just one."

"I'll be expecting you on the executive floor in half an hour. Be on time this time."

I hung up before she could answer. If she was as desperate as she sounded, she would be right on time. Then I turned apologetically to my friends.

"I have to go. Something business-related."

Chapter Five: Do You Dare, Little Dove?

Blossom

It was the first time I'd ever missed a shift at the Royal Red, but special circumstances called for special measures. I had no clue what exactly Nolan wanted from me, or why he had ordered me to the executive floor of Caldwell Industries.

But if there was anything I could do to turn the tide, I would do it.

After giving my name at the reception desk, I was immediately taken to a private elevator, which took me directly to the executive floor.

At least there were no more stairs. As of this morning, I'd had enough stairs. At least for the next three years, maybe even forever.

The closer I got to the executive floor, the more restlessly my heart was beating in my chest. And when I got out of the elevator and saw about three dozen applicants waiting outside the office, I swallowed hard.

I could have been sitting there if I hadn't blown it yesterday. I felt insecure, especially because I stood out like a sore thumb in the red silk dress I always wore at the Royal Red. It had a wide cut at the side so that I could sit comfortably and play well, and for the first time I felt naked because half my thigh was flashing out.

The dress code of the other women was also elegant in a business casual sort of way, and they all seemed to have learned their makeup from the same YouTube tutorial I had failed at. Apart from some lipstick and blush, I wore nothing, because in my twenty-two years of life I had never once managed to draw two eyeliner lines of the same length. Even Ruby had despaired of me when she tried, and her eyeliner was always perfect.

"Blossom." Nolan suddenly stood in front of me, looking down at me appraisingly. In his hand he held the application form I had handed in at reception. He turned to the other women, who were all staring at him with wide eyes.

Frowning, I watched as they batted their eyelashes in such a way that I could hear Ruby's cynical voice in the back of my head, or bit their lower lips.

"You can go, ladies," he said. Then he paid no more attention to the other women and looked at me. "Come along."

I followed him uncertainly, because I still didn't know what to expect. I felt death stares on my back, because the gathered women clearly thought I had cheated them out of their jobs. But it could just as well be that he was only sending the women away so that no one could hear him loudly telling me off for not being able to pay my debts.

I got all giddy when I walked into the office labeled "Nolan Caldwell".

I faltered. "This is your office?"

"This isn't just my office, it's my company," he replied coolly. His hard gaze grazed me, then he closed the door behind me, forcing me to inhale his perfume. Sandalwood, with a hint of bourbon.

"I didn't know that," I replied, because I didn't know what else to say.

"You might have known if you hadn't just walked away this morning." His jaws ground together, a sign that he was still angry about our last encounter. Could I blame him? No, but knowing my situation, you couldn't blame me for acting the way I did.

"I'm sorry, but I had my reasons," I began.

"I don't care about your reasons," he cut me off as he sat down in an office chair so obnoxiously large that it resembled a throne.

I bit my tongue so as not to say the wrong thing.

"When are you planning to pay off your debt?" He seemed to have a penchant for getting to the point.

"As soon as possible. Once I have a job again, then..."

Again he cut me off and it took all the nerve I had not to snort.

"*If* you get another job," he said matter-of-factly. He didn't seem to trust my abilities or my willpower, which was sobering. I shouldn't care what he thought of me, but it still hurt.

"I'll find a job, I promise. You don't know me, but I keep my promises."

He merely looked at me in silence, as if he knew something about me that I didn't.

I tilted my head to the side to push my loose hair out of my face, secretly rolling my eyes to relieve my frustration.

"I saw that," he growled, and my body immediately reacted with goosebumps.

"What do you want from me?" I asked after I couldn't stand his gaze any longer and stared in the other direction.

"I want you to apologize." His expression became so serious that I could see the sternness out of the corner of my eye. He was angry, furious even.

"For the accident?" I asked cautiously, already thinking up soothing words. After all, I was working on making up for the mistake.

"For rolling your eyes," he growled.

I blinked at him in surprise. "I'm sorry," I replied, although I wasn't really sorry. He had provoked me, and apart from that it wasn't a crime to move my eyes.

Nolan stood up and came toward me. To my shame, I backed away until I bumped into the wall behind me.

"Maybe you'll give it another sincere try," he breathed against my lips. His breath tickled my skin and the scent of bourbon clouded my senses.

My heart was racing and my body was shaking. I knew these symptoms, but not in this context. I felt good about it, in a twisted way. My whole body was shaking, and I wanted more of it. What was wrong with me?

In my mind, I repeated the phrases I always listed when I wanted to distract myself.

"Columba livia," slipped quietly from my lips.

He looked at me questioningly. "What does that mean?"

"It's the Latin name for a city pigeon," I replied, hoping he wouldn't ask for an explanation, because the explanation would raise even more questions.

"Interesting, little dove." He brushed a strand of hair behind my ear and his lips came closer and closer. I held my breath, hoping he'd go through with whatever he was about to do, but at the last moment he pushed off against the wall behind me and ran back to the other end of the office.

"Apologize," Nolan demanded once more. There was something harsh in his voice that I couldn't quite interpret. Was he angry again?

"Sorry," I replied and joined him. But because my body was still electrified, I couldn't sit down on the armchair in front of his desk.

"Better." He nodded. "And now let's talk about how you can pay off your debt to me."

He opened my application folder without reading it.

"You studied at the University of Seattle. A good school," he said, going through my resume. I nodded, and my heart tightened briefly because I knew what he was going to ask next.

"Why did you drop out? Your grades were excellent, you only needed one more semester and you would have had a flourishing career as a pianist."

"I can't play anymore," I replied curtly.

"You play at the Royal Red." He still pronounced the name as if it were a shed where only dubious types hung out for illegal gambling and prostitution.

"That's something else," I rebutted. "It's... a different league from playing professionally."

Why did the one topic I didn't want to talk about have to be revisited again and again? I was tired of it.

I rubbed my right arm and pulled the sleeve of my dress further over my wrist.

"Your second major was computer science," he continued. I was infinitely grateful to him for that. Although I doubted it was due to his immense empathy that he had noticed how uncomfortable I felt about the subject. It was probably more down to his pragmatism in getting through the items on the agenda as quickly as possible.

"Yes, that's why I'm more than qualified for the job," I replied very slowly. I had hated computer science, but I was grateful to my parents for persuading me to take a second subject as security.

"What brought you to New York?" Nolan asked, continuing to poke into my private life. His eyes scrutinized me and I got the feeling that he was trying to read my mind.

"I needed a change of scenery," I lied with a laugh. It wasn't a change of scenery; I had blown up my old life and burned all the bridges leading back to Seattle.

Fuck Seattle.

"Good, you're hired." He looked at me seriously.

"Really?" I blinked at him in disbelief, expecting him to pull the same stunt as his coworker, certain that dashing hopes was company policy, but he remained serious.

"Yes, really. But I don't want to see any more rolled eyes, otherwise we'll have a problem."

My heart skipped a beat, and I had to stop myself from jumping into his arms and hugging him with gratitude. Only my gut feeling, which said that this man wasn't the huggy type, stopped me.

"No more rolling my eyes," I assured him, nodding.

"And not another word about stupid rules. You don't know me, but you'll get to know me—me and my rules, which I set great store by."

"The man who coordinated the applications told you about me?" I asked in surprise. The guy had screamed brownnoser, just by the way he had adjusted his glasses.

"Yes."

I wondered whether it was a good or a bad sign that I had stuck in the employee's mind and whether it would affect my future work.

"No more rule hating, I promise." I put a hand on my chest to emphasize the words, and Nolan looked at me with a critical expression.

"You shouldn't make promises so lightly that you might not be able to keep." He spoke the words carefully, almost reverently, and goosebumps crawled down my spine.

"I will keep my promises. You've given me a job that will save my ass. I'd do anything for it." Thanks to him, I wouldn't be on the street next month, so I resolved to be the best assistant he'd ever had, to show my appreciation.

"I didn't do it out of charity, Blossom, but because it's the easiest way to pay your debt to me," he explained matter-of-factly, depriving me of the illusion that he perhaps did have a heart.

"Sure, of course." Embarrassed, I avoided his gaze. He was right. It was a tough business deal between us, and all the emotions I thought I saw in him were just my imagination.

He walked around his desk once more and looked deep into my eyes.

"You said you'd do anything," he whispered. My knees went weak again. So weak that I had to lean on his desk to keep from falling over.

"That was just something I said." My voice was no more than a whisper.

"It's dangerous to just say things with me. I take things very seriously, which means I will always take you at your word."

It sounded like a threat, and one that made my body vibrate.

"I'll remember that, Nolan." Unconsciously, I started picking at my nails, like I always did when I was nervous.

His eyes narrowed for half a second. "I'll remember that, *sir*."

I corrected myself, to which he smiled in satisfaction.

"When we're alone, you can keep calling me Nolan," he said, and I nodded.

He pulled a stack of papers from one of the drawers, which he placed in front of me while he made himself comfortable in his chair and watched me.

"Read through and sign," he demanded in a serious tone. My eyes widened as I estimated that I had half a book to read through before I could sign the employment contract.

I skimmed over the most important things, then reached out for a pen because I wanted to sign as quickly as possible. With a starting salary of forty thousand dollars, I couldn't do anything to risk not being hired after all.

"You really should read through everything." He looked at me reprovingly.

"I've skimmed through everything, and I'm satisfied. It's only about my job, not my soul," I replied with a smile.

He handed me his pen, and as he stared at my hand he growled softly. "That awful nail polish will be gone by tomorrow."

"This is Magic Red Velvet," I started to explain, but he cut me off.

"I don't care if it's what Oprah recommends, my personal assistants don't wear hooker red."

"The same hooker red as your car?" I teased, because my bruised pride felt cornered. Of course, I immediately regretted my words, but I couldn't take them back. And also I was right. My nail polish was the same color as his car. The one that had forced me into this job forever.

"And I don't want you to wear that dress anymore, it's far too revealing," Nolan continued, as if I hadn't raised any objections.

I anxiously smoothed the creases out of the smooth fabric and looked down at myself. It wasn't Gucci, it was just an off-the-rack dress, but I still liked it. It was one of the few elegant dresses with long sleeves available in my price range.

"But I always wear it when I'm working. I don't have any other dress. And I like it," I replied.

Nolan pulled a credit card out of his wallet. "Then buy yourself another one that you'll like even more without attracting the attention of every man in the room. On my tab."

I waved my hands emphatically. "I can't and won't accept that."

"If you want to work for me, you will." He raised a brow in reprove. I realized that Nolan wasn't used to people turning down his offers.

I reluctantly took the credit card with the intention of never using it. He wouldn't even notice a few double-digit movements on his account, and I could simply claim that I had bought another evening dress.

"Thank you," I replied, trying not to sound as pained as I felt. "If there's nothing else, I need to go back to my other job now." I pointed to the door.

"Not in that outfit," he grumbled.

"Like I said, I don't have anything else. But I could perform naked."

His eyes darkened and he opened his drawer once more.

"You could work off your debt to me twice as fast," he said, his voice sounding as guttural as a hungry wolf. He slid another contract across the table, but before I could take it, he pulled it back. "You should read this contract word for word."

Getting rid of the debt twice as fast sounded good, but his grim expression said everything I needed to know. There was a huge catch. And when I read the first lines of the contract I recoiled, because I discovered the catch. He wanted me to submit to him in a way that made my skin tingle.

"Thanks, but no thanks. I'm more than happy with the job as a personal assistant," I replied hoarsely. Actually, I should be upset about the offer, but I felt weirdly flattered. But it wasn't a good idea at all, I knew that.

My wildest relationship was holding hands, and my wildest sexual experience was kissing Rachel Miller while playing spin-the-bottle under the football bleachers at my old high school. I'd been too much of a goody-two-shoes for anything else. And after leaving Seattle, I had sworn off relationships altogether.

Nolan leaned forward. "I'll double the price."

Considering the huge sum, I did think about his offer. But what were the chances that he would be happy with me, considering I had zero experience? I was still a virgin, and for good reason. But there was no way I was going to turn him against me, until at least the costs of the accident were paid.

"I'm afraid I'm not qualified enough for this. You've already emphasized that it's pretty important to you," I said, feeling like a rhetorical genius for using his own words against him.

"I decide who is qualified and who is not." He put the pen back on the paper and looked at me expectantly. "Sign if you dare, little dove."

Chapter Six: How Much is a Promise Worth in Your World?

Nolan

I pressed the button to the intercom that connected me to Blossom's desk.

"A coffee." Then I let go of the button and went back to my work. Or at least I tried to, but I couldn't finish any of my thoughts. My eyes kept glancing at my new assistant, who was now standing up from her desk, which was right in front of my glass wall.

She was wearing a gray skirt and a white blouse that was tied closed at the neck with a wide bow. Her outfit screamed "good girl" so much that I wanted to grab her and throw her over the table, because good girls always secretly want it the hardest. Just like that. Now. And when she walked into the office with a steaming cup of coffee, I was about to do it.

"Your coffee." Smiling, she put the cup down on my desk and waited for further instructions.

"I want a coffee from Daisy's," I said tonelessly. Her features slipped for a second before she regained her composure and nodded.

"Coming right up." She bit her lips to keep a curse from slipping out, but I knew what was going on in that pretty little head of hers. She hated me for treating her unfairly.

Maybe I was treating her unfairly, but only because she wouldn't sign my contract. She had been the first to turn down my offer, and that made me furious.

The more she resisted, the more I wanted to possess her, and her treacherous body signaled to me that she felt the same way. She wanted it to, she just couldn't admit it.

I immersed myself in my work until Blossom came back with a to-go cup from Daisy's and placed it on the desk for me. She tried to hide how fast she was breathing, but failed.

Her body trembled and I had to seriously restrain myself to keep from losing control. Of course, I knew the attraction was just because she was new and untasted; rationally I understood it.

But my thought processes had been anything but rational. I could only think of two things:

Was she a good girl or a bad girl, and how could I punish her for it?

By the time she had signed the contract, the allure of her untouchability would have worn off. I was sure of it.

"Thank you," I replied, turning my gaze away from her.

"Is there anything else you need?" She smiled at me, almost victoriously, thinking that she had done a good job that didn't provide a target for new criticism, and she was right. I couldn't criticize her work, but that didn't mean I had nothing to say.

"Did you buy a new dress?" I asked.

She blinked at me in surprise. She obviously hadn't been prepared for this question. All the better for me, because it made it easier for me to read the truth from her face.

"Why do you ask?" She avoided my question, which was answer enough for me. To be more precise, she not only avoided my question, but also my gaze, which spoke volumes.

"Because I told you to. So?" I stood up and looked at her expectantly, standing close enough that she was forced to return my gaze.

"Yes, I did." She rolled her eyes and was about to leave, but I followed her and braced my hand against the door as she tried to open it.

"You're a bad liar," I growled. I tried not to take it personally that she was lying to me. She didn't have bad intentions, she was just insecure.

"I haven't had time to buy a new dress yet," she replied, avoiding my gaze again.

"Blossom." Just saying her name was enough to show her that she might be able to play this game with others, but not with me.

"I like my dress." Now she was finally telling the truth as she returned my gaze.

"There. Was that so hard?" I asked.

She shook her head, and I had to suppress the urge to run my fingers through her loose hair.

"In future, you should tie your hair in a braid." My hands clenched into fists as it became harder and harder to resist the urge. I wanted to grab her by that gorgeous head of hair, bend her over the table, and do unspeakable things to her.

"Why?" she asked innocently, as if she didn't know what I thought about her. But she should know. No one was as innocent as Blossom was. And no one could misinterpret my damn looks. I didn't know why I couldn't control myself around her, but I couldn't help it.

"It's more practical," I replied after a long pause.

"My loose hair doesn't bother me." She ran her hand through the ends of her hair, which was long enough to fall over her breasts.

"Do I have to write it in the employment contract?" I raised a brow in rebuke because she had contradicted me. Again.

So much rule-breaking, and no way to punish her for it...

"You settle everything with a contract, don't you?" She tilted her head and looked at me reproachfully. I wanted to push her against my desk and fuck that expression off her face.

"Why not?" I countered.

She continued to dig deeper. "If you force everyone to do everything, how much is a promise worth?" Her green eyes were rimmed with hazel brown; they pierced me in a way that made me uncomfortable.

"Promises aren't worth anything," I growled and turned away from her. I'd broken enough promises in my life to know what I was talking about.

"In a world ruled by money, I guess not," she muttered. She was about to leave when I wheeled around to face her again. I grabbed her wrist and pressed her against the wall. Our bodies touched, reacted, collided.

Fuck. This was going too far, but I still couldn't stop.

"You have no idea what my world is about." My jaws ground tightly together, because I was sick of the world I was talking about. Even custom made suits and *Times* puff pieces didn't hide where I was coming from.

"That's right, you're not letting anyone in on it." Blossom tried to suppress her snort, but failed miserably.

"For good reason," I replied coolly.

"Oh yeah?" She looked at me provocatively, almost defiantly. But if she thought I was going to perform a soul striptease, she was wrong. I didn't share my feelings, especially not with a sub.

She's not your sub, my subconscious snarled at me. That didn't change the fact that I wanted her.

"If you expect an answer from me, we should clarify once again where your place is, little dove." I pressed myself even harder against her, causing her to gasp. She couldn't deny the effect I was having on her body, but she still glared at me angrily.

"Where is my place?" she asked.

I was thrown off balance. It wasn't the question, but the way she looked at me. I had the feeling that she was literally begging me to put her in her place, to show her where her place was in my world. In front of me, naked, on her knees.

"Sign the contract and I'll show you," I whispered in her ear.

"I can't," she replied quietly.

"Why?" My hand wandered up her arm until I reached her neck. Her heart was beating so wildly that I could feel her pulse. My thumb grazed her lower lip, and she willingly opened her mouth.

Damn, this is getting out of hand!

"Sign. The. Contract." My tone was insistent enough to make her entire body tremble. She pressed her pelvis against me, and her begging look told me everything I needed to know. Blossom wanted me to subdue her, and I had no idea what was standing in the way of that.

Our lips were about to touch when she shook her head and opened her mouth to contradict me, even though her body was sending clear signals. Then I did something I knew I would regret.

I silenced her with a kiss. Not a bland, simple kiss, but one that took her breath away. She moaned against my lips, tempting me to go further. My hand touched her cheek and my tongue flicked over her lower lip, begging to explore her mouth.

Vanilla mixed with the even sweeter taste of innocence almost drove me out of my mind.

"You could get more," I said between kisses that left her breathless.

"More," she replied with a soft sigh. A smile appeared on her lips as she pressed herself toward me.

"All you have to do is sign. We're already going way too far." My tone was insistent, but my hands didn't want to let go of her delicate body.

"I want you," she whispered softly. A groan escaped my throat. "But I want *you*. No contract, no rules. This feels wrong."

She shook her head and I took a step back, because I could no longer guarantee that I would remain a gentleman if I had to breathe in vanilla and innocence any longer.

"No, don't stop," she begged softly, clutching my jacket.

"I could go on." My fingers ran along her cheek. "But only with a contract."

She inhaled sharply, then her face hardened. "Fine, then don't."

Her pride was tarnished, but that was nothing compared to my pride because she kept turning down my damn offers. I could lay the world at her feet, all she had to do was get down on her knees in front of me. Deep in her heart, she longed for it. She might be able to fool herself, but not me. I recognized a woman who longed for submission, and Blossom was crying out to be dominated.

"Tie back your hair starting tomorrow," I grumbled. It was a stupid idea not to fire her on the spot, but I wanted to find out how far we could both take this game before it escalated to a dangerous level.

"Fine by me." Without making a face, she tossed her hair over her shoulder.

"And you will get yourself another evening dress. I never want to see you in that red dress again," I demanded.

She sighed softly, then gave me a questioning look. "Why do you keep criticizing me?"

Something flashed in her eyes that looked like pain, but I didn't want to acknowledge it. Had I caused it? Shit, of course. Besides, why couldn't I stop criticizing her? When did I become this kind of person?

"Daisy's coffee was good," I finally replied.

She put her hands on her hips. "Thank you. But it's a little late."

"Do you want me to praise you for everything that's part of your job? If you want to hear that you're a good girl, you'll have to impress me with other things."

Her eyes widened for a fraction of a second before she dropped her gaze.

"I don't expect praise, but your criticism is hurtful." She rubbed her right arm until she realized I was watching her. Then she reflexively hid both arms behind her back.

"My criticism was appropriate," I replied calmly.

"But you're not criticizing my work, you're criticizing things that don't concern you at all. My dress, for example. Even if you think it's awful, it's not your place to judge it. And you certainly can't take the liberty of forbidding me to wear it, even if you hate it."

The opposite was the case; I thought the dress was beautiful. And that's exactly why I didn't want her to wear it. In that long red silk dress, she was crying out to be fucked, and I couldn't bear the thought that another man might take her outfit as an invitation.

"Wear something else or I'll consider our working relationship history," I barked. "And if you're going shopping anyway, get yourself another outfit for this job."

Blossom bit her lips, then took a deep breath.

"How about you choose an outfit for me, because I obviously can't do anything right for you?"

"Good point." I sat back in my seat. "You can go now. I have a meeting in a minute."

Chapter Seven: Streptopelia Turtur. Columba Livia. Streptopelia Decaocto

Blossom

Wearing a braid was unusual, but I didn't want to start another argument with my new boss that would jeopardize my job. Today, on my second day at work, I was determined not to give him a single chance to criticize me.

And to make sure nothing went wrong, I was in the office an hour earlier than necessary to get ready. To my surprise, Nolan was already there, or still there, working his way through a huge pile of documents.

When he noticed me, he waved me into the office.

"You're early," he said, and I was almost certain his tone was reproachful.

"You don't like unpunctuality," I replied calmly, hoping I was sending the right signals. I wanted to do everything right today and not upset him.

I briefly questioned my true ambitions. Was I just trying to do a good job, or was I just having a hard time coping with him looking at me as if I had somehow set his company on fire?

"That's right, I hate being late. But I like it when I have my peace and quiet in the morning."

I was an expert at making myself invisible; I never liked being the center of attention. Still, his answer gave me a little stab in the heart because I just couldn't bring myself to do, or not do, anything that would upset him.

"You won't even notice me," I replied with a shrug, because it really wasn't a big deal for me to fade into the background. Even on stage, the focus was not on me, but on my music.

"I doubt that." He gave me a strange look that I couldn't interpret. "You should change your clothes."

At my questioning look, he pointed to my chair, over the back of which hung a bulky dry cleaning bag.

"You really got me clothes?" I stared open-mouthed at the garments, and then back at Nolan.

"You sound surprised." He casually put his hands in his pockets while he looked at me appraisingly.

"I am surprised," I replied, nodding and wondering which of us was the weird one in this situation.

Him, because he really kept his word, or me, because I came from a world where it wasn't normal to spend hundreds of dollars on an outfit.

"You should know by now that you can take me at my word," he emphasized seriously.

"I'll keep that in mind, sir," I replied, nodding.

"Good girl," he growled, so quietly that I wasn't sure if he had really said it. Part of me wished it was true, while the rest of me shook my head reprovingly.

What was it about this man, his solitary, unfriendly, and sometimes hurtful manner, and the fact I was attracted to it? Was my taste in men really that broken? Was *I* that broken?

"I'm going to change," I said, breaking the long wall of silence I had built up around myself.

"Go ahead." He pointed to the exit and I forced my body to finally get moving. I took the outfit, which consisted of a skirt and top, and disappeared into the bathroom.

"Please let it be too big or too small," I whispered to the fabric. Nolan always acted as if he was infallible, and this would be the perfect moment to prove him wrong. But fate didn't grant me that much luck, because the clothes fit so perfectly that I wondered how long he had stared at me to be able to know my measurements.

I looked elegant, but also so innocent that even my virginity took pity and wanted to tip a large portion of Magic Red Velvet nail polish over the fabric.

Even though I knew Ruby would tease me about it for the next few weeks, I sent her a selfie.

BLOSSOM: Welcome to Caldwell Industries. How can I help?

RUBY: Holy crap.

BLOSSOM: Thank you, you really build me up.

RUBY: Your outfit screams weird kinks.

BLOSSOM: Ruby! You are impossible.

I gasped and my cheeks turned a deep red because our conversation was going in a direction I didn't like. Which didn't necessarily mean that Ruby was wrong. In fact, she was probably right in her assumption, considering the contract Nolan had presented me with the other day.

Just thinking about it made my skin prickle, and I wondered if I shouldn't sign the contract after all. Just to pay off my debts even faster, of course, so that I wouldn't have to work for Mr. Icecold any longer than necessary.

At least that's what I told myself. It had absolutely nothing to do with his broad shoulders, or the husky voice that made my heart flutter.

RUBY: Okay, then it doesn't scream crazy preferences, it screams the urge to want to protect your virginity at all costs.

I rolled my eyes and stuffed my phone back into my shoulder bag. My innocence was the main reason I hadn't read through the contract in the first place. Nolan was already unhappy with the things I had studied. I wonder how he would react to things I'd never done before.

I returned to my seat and dedicated myself to organizing the day's events. Nolan's next appointment was at Mercer Solutions at the other end of Manhattan. It was most likely about the merger of three companies that he was currently working on, and I smiled with satisfaction. It would be pretty quiet in the boardroom due to his absence.

My phone buzzed. Nolan was still engrossed in his work, so I risked a glance.

RUBY: You know what's even worse than your outfit?

RUBY: When you ghost me.

BLOSSOM: I'm not ignoring you

BLOSSOM: I just don't have anything to say about it

"Are you bored with your work?" a voice asked from behind me.

I winced and dropped my phone in shock, but thanks to my protective kitten cover, the screen remained intact.

"No, not at all," I replied, shaking my head. "That was just my girlfriend, Ruby. She was curious about my new outfit."

I was babbling, which didn't make my situation any better.

"Leave your phone here, I don't need any distractions," Nolan said tonelessly, walking ahead of me. He didn't look back to make sure I was following him. He just expected me to, and because I needed this job, I had to follow him.

"I don't quite understand," I said, jumping up from my seat and trotting after him.

"You're coming with me." He gave me a quick glance to make sure I'd understood him. And because I had no other choice, I nodded, but couldn't stop myself from asking why he expected me to.

"Why?" I asked, trying to hide my disappointment that I wouldn't have the executive floor to myself after all.

"Because it's your job," he replied dryly. He got into the elevator without giving me a chance to pack anything I might need for the meeting. Hopefully Mercer Solutions had all the documents, otherwise my plan to do a perfect job today would fail in the first hour.

As the elevator doors closed, Nolan looked at me urgently. "Why are you doing this job?"

I returned his gaze and stood up to him as best I could. I leaned against the gray metal wall, because the quick descent made my knees weak.

"To pay off my debts," I answered honestly.

"You know very well that I meant something else." He kept his serious expression, but I could hear genuine interest in his voice. That made it all the worse, because he only seemed interested in the one subject I didn't want to talk about.

I didn't have to look at the clock to know that the journey would take longer than I would have liked.

"Then what do you mean instead?" I asked innocently. Of course I knew he was talking about me dropping out of university, but I still hoped he wouldn't bring it up. But my boss wasn't just my boss, he was a sadist who had decided to drive me mad whenever he could.

"Blossom." His face darkened. He really wasn't used to being contradicted.

"If you're worried that I'm suddenly going to have a change of heart and go back to university, I can reassure you. I've already told you that I can't keep up the standard." I bit my lips and breathed in deeply through my nose to push back the queasy feeling that was spreading through my body.

Of course I wanted to be strong, but with this one topic that I couldn't even talk about in my head, my nerves were immediately on edge.

"I didn't mean to offend you," Nolan said tonelessly, but his eyes betrayed for a split second that he wasn't as cold as he usually was. "I just wanted to make sure you had the same ambitions in your current job."

"That almost sounded like an apology," I said. Then I smiled to show that I wasn't holding a grudge. Apart from that, debts in the dizzyingly high range were a huge motivator for mere mortals.

"Don't make a fool of yourself," he growled.

Then the elevator doors to the underground car park opened and I followed him. His replacement car was a black Porsche parked next to my bike. At least the black car didn't give me the idea of tipping Ruby's bright red nail polish over the hood in case something went wrong.

Just as I was about to go to my Honda to get out my helmet and protective gear, he opened the passenger door of his car and whistled for me to come over.

"You're coming with me." It wasn't an invitation, it was an order.

Swallowing hard, I complied with his request. It took a lot of effort to get into the car, but I managed it. My therapist, Rhyan, would have been proud of me, because I hadn't managed to get into a car once in Seattle. Not even after months of therapy, even though he was a pretty good therapist.

But when I closed the door, I felt like I was in a tiny little cage. One that was getting smaller and smaller, and could crash into the nearest wall at a hundred speeds.

Streptopelia turtur. Columba livia. Streptopelia decaocto.

"The seatbelt," Nolan said shortly.

I grasped the belt; it felt like a noose around my neck. I pulled it forward a few inches, but then stopped. I just couldn't manage to chain myself to the vehicle with it.

No matter how many bird names I recited in my mind, fear clutched my stomach with ice-cold hands until I stood up and fled the car in panic.

Nolan didn't say a word, just stared at me uncomprehendingly, which made things even worse.

"I'm sorry, I can't," I said, breathing heavily and fighting against fainting. To distract myself, I pulled on my helmet and leathers before he had a chance to ask why I was panicking.

Over the last few years, I had perfected putting on my protective gear, and it didn't take me fifteen seconds.

"I'll see you at Mercer Solutions," I said, then I jumped on my bike and sped away from the situation as fast as the speed limit would allow.

Streptopelia turtur. Columba livia. Streptopelia decaocto.
Streptopelia turtur. Columba livia. Streptopelia decaocto.
Streptopelia turtur. Columba livia. Streptopelia decaocto.

Chapter Eight: You'll Have to Think About Me All Day

Blossom

I arrived in the lobby of Mercer Solution ten minutes before Nolan. In the meantime, I obtained the documents I needed for the meeting.

But his dark look as he entered the hall sent an icy shiver down my spine. He was angry. Not just a little, but spoiled-milk sour.

I could hardly expect praise for my foresight with the documents. I was more likely to be criticized because I had stormed off earlier. Admittedly, not a very clever move, but better than bursting into tears in front of him because I had opened up old wounds that never healed properly.

"That was unprofessional," he barked as he walked past me to the elevators.

"I'm really sorry. Cars and I..." I began to explain ruefully what was going on inside me, but he cut me off.

"I don't care what your problem with cars is, Blossom." The way he pronounced my name made me swallow hard.

"I wish I could say it would never happen again, but I can't." I forced myself to keep looking at him, even though I wanted to sink through the ground in shame. Even though he made it anything but easy for me, I wanted to do my job well. If only so that Little Miss Scratchy and I didn't end up on the street.

He returned my gaze. His jaw was tense, and I got the feeling that today would be my last day working for him, but he didn't say anything, just got into the elevator when the doors opened.

"What are you waiting for?" he asked me, because I was frozen to a pillar of salt.

I immediately shook my legs awake and followed him. He pressed the button for the executive floor and I braced myself for a long ride up.

"If you leave me like that again, you're fired," Nolan said out of nowhere.

I took a breath to object, but he raised a finger. "I don't expect your problem to be solved tomorrow, but I do expect you to solve it."

I nodded, even though I had no idea how to comply with his request. This wasn't about a different hairstyle or new clothes, but about the greatest fear I had ever felt in my life.

The longer I looked at him, the more certain I was that his demand was not about work.

"What is this really about?" I asked, so as not to have to ponder forever what he really wanted.

"Huh?" He raised a brow questioningly and leaned against the chrome wall of the elevator.

"That I sort out the car thing. It's not about me doing my job, is it?"

"What else would I be talking about?" He looked at me as if I had lost my mind. Not because I was wrong, but because I was right, and had brought it up, and now he was uncomfortable with that fact.

"Just a thought," I replied with a shrug.

"You should keep your thoughts to yourself in future," he whispered.

"I just thought..."

He cut me off again. "Never mind."

Take a deep breath. Don't do anything you might regret later. My subconscious bombarded me with every mindfulness mantra I'd ever picked up, but I couldn't keep my thoughts to myself.

"You don't have to patronize me like that. I'd do a good and conscientious job even if we were friends."

"Friends." He spat out the words as if they were bitter as bile. "You and I could never be friends."

I bit my lip to hold back what I actually had to say. He seemed to think he was better than me. Yes, we came from different worlds, and yes, I was just his assistant. But that didn't mean he could treat me the way he did.

"Why not?" I asked as calmly as I could.

"Because I don't need friends." His tone left no doubt that he meant it. For the first time since I'd known him, I felt sorry for him. To sum up, I may have had less money at the end of the month, but I also had friends who always had my back when it mattered. Without Vince and Ruby, I really would have been up a creek. Just the thought that Nolan had no one to rely on made it pretty hard for me to keep hating him.

"Anyone who says something like that needs a friend all the more," I said quietly.

"You and me are not going to be friends," he repeated his words with a growl.

Before I could demand an explanation he turned to me, grabbed me by the shoulders, and pressed me against the wall of the elevator.

"We could be something other than friends, if you would sign the contract. I'm not capable of anything else." His breath tickled my neck, raising goosebumps. The rough shadow of his beard rubbed across my skin and if he hadn't pushed me against the wall, I would have keeled over, because his words had melted my kneecaps.

He's no good for you.

I realized that I had terrible taste in men, and that no matter what I did, I would only disappoint him further. I wanted my first time to be memorable because it was good, because it felt right, not because my outrageously handsome boss gave me a bad grade. Nevertheless, my body reacted differently than I would have liked.

"I can't." Shaking my head, I wanted to turn away from him, but his engaging manner prevented me from doing so.

"Yes, you could. You just don't want to, there's a huge difference," he replied with a low chuckle. It was the first time I'd ever heard him laugh.

"I would only disappoint you," I replied with a sigh. I should tell him I was a virgin, and then he would stop playing this game with me, but I just couldn't. Part of me wanted him to keep showing interest in me, because I liked the feeling.

I hadn't let anyone get close to me since college, and it was probably a stupid idea that would end in heartbreak, but I couldn't help it. Besides, Nolan would soon lose interest anyway. After all, he could have anyone, with his broad shoulders and I-get-what-I-want expression.

"How do you know what would be a disappointment for me?" he asked, snapping me out of my thoughts.

I knew nothing—that was exactly the problem. I was a virgin, and apart from knowledge gathered from a few spicy novels, I knew nothing about what he had planned for me.

"I just know it."

His hands grabbed my wrists and held them above my head. When his eyes darkened, my whole body shook.

"You should be careful with such claims, little dove. Especially with claims that concern me. You know nothing about me."

"Maybe that's the problem?" I asked as I tried to get a grip on my fluttering breath.

"The problem is that you won't sign the damn contract," he whispered calmly, but his eyes blazed with anger. I could see he was fighting with every fiber of his being to control himself.

"That's why you hate me, isn't it?" The question slipped past my lips unintentionally, because it was just a thought that had just occurred to me.

"I don't hate you," he replied.

I blinked in surprise. "Then you're just punishing me. It's the same thing." I looked at him challengingly, thinking that I could compete with him. But I had never been so wrong in my life.

"Absolutely not. If I hated you, I would destroy you, little dove. I would destroy you until there was nothing left of you to destroy. You have no idea how deep my boundless hatred can go."

I believed every word he said, and the rage that resonated in his words made my breath catch. Whoever this anger was directed at... I didn't want to change places with that person.

He held me in place with his left hand while his right hand wandered along my body. He stroked my cheek, my neck, my collarbone. And although he didn't touch a single indecent area—areas that no one had ever touched before, mind you—my heart raced and beat wildly against my ribs.

"You'd know if I hated you." His finger slid over my bottom lip, making me open my mouth willingly. Whatever was happening was escalating. My control was slipping away, and the worst part was that I liked it.

More. I wanted more of it. So much more that I had to ask myself whether I had lost my mind.

"Then why do you want to punish me?" I asked innocently, because I wanted to hear what he was thinking.

"Don't push your luck, little dove," he whispered in my ear. I tried to suppress my sigh, but I failed. The situation was far too exciting, far too forbidden to stop now. I pressed myself against his body, and felt him tense up.

"Don't challenge me," Nolan commanded in a throaty voice, but my body no longer obeyed me. I jutted my chin out so that our lips were almost touching; I could already taste bourbon and masculinity on my tongue.

Something dark flashed in his eyes. "Fine, you wouldn't have it any other way."

He took my breath away with a kiss and my body exploded. Within that moment, Nolan burned himself into my memory forever, because there was no question that I could ever forget that kiss. For the first time in my life, he made me feel something other than fear, and it felt pretty good.

His hand slipped under my skirt and I groaned as he touched the hem of my panties. But instead of massaging the spot that was throbbing with pleasure and demanding release, he took off my panties and put them in his pants pocket. Then he moved away, and where his body had been he left behind nothing but an empty coldness that made me shiver.

It took me a moment to collect myself and realize what had just happened. Without underwear, I felt strangely naked, which was humiliating in a way that made heat rush to my cheeks, because I secretly liked it.

"My underwear," I insisted, holding out my hand.

"My subs never demand anything from me," he replied tonelessly. His neutral, serious expression had returned, but his eyes were still burning with the fire whose sparks had jumped over to me.

"I'm not your sub," I replied, leaving my hand outstretched.

"But you want to be punished by me," he concluded correctly. Or at least half-right. I had challenged him, true, because I wanted to know how far he would go, but only because I'd never expected it to get so out of hand.

"Yes. You put me in my place, I get it." I wanted to roll my eyes, but I remembered how sensitively he had reacted to that last time, so I snorted softly instead.

"You haven't understood anything yet. But you will. With every step you take today, you'll feel how much power I can have over you, little dove. You will think of me with every step you take, and with every damn step you take you will crave more of my dominance."

He was serious. Only after the elevator doors opened and we left the small enclosed space that I realized just how serious. My heart fluttered excitedly. I should hate him, from the bottom of my heart, because he didn't show me any other feelings either, but I couldn't.

A small, rather broken part of me wanted to find out if he would go any further, if he could make my heart beat even more wildly.

"All right, I'll play along. When do I get my panties back?" I asked, crossing my arms in front of my chest.

Nolan drew close to me. "When you've learned that people don't just leave me like that. Not in the parking garage, not after you've scratched my car. You don't know me well yet, but this should demonstrate to you that I can get pretty damn uncomfortable."

It wasn't a warning, but a crystal-clear threat that made my abdomen tremble.

What's wrong with me? I had never acted like this before. The world had changed since I turned my back on Seattle.

No, the world was still the same old cruel world. I had changed. But that wasn't quite true either, because where Nolan reached me, in the deepest depths of my forbidden fantasies, nothing had changed since I had first looked into those dark abysses.

"Blossom." He stood in the hall, tapping his foot impatiently. "Do I really need to take more clothes off you to illustrate that I hate being left standing?"

I winced because he had caught me daydreaming. "No, sorry." I quickly followed him down the corridor.

"No, *sir*," he corrected me, and the vibrating undertone in his voice told me that in some twisted, perhaps even forbidden way, he liked it when I knew where my position was. Somewhere far, far below him.

"Understood," I replied, nodding, and when his expression darkened, I hastily added a "sir".

Good God. Just the thought of being trapped in a room with him for the next few hours and having to think about him every second made me jittery.

What had I gotten myself into?

Chapter Nine: You Write to Me Every Evening. Without Exception

Nolan

After the business meeting we stopped at Daisy's, because I hadn't eaten since the morning.

I had no idea why Blossom didn't want to get into my car, but that had to change. It wasn't just about professionalism, it was about keeping control, and I didn't have that if I didn't have her in sight.

This time I was there earlier than her, and when she entered the café I got up to help her out of the leather jacket she was still wearing. She must have seen me through the window, otherwise she would have taken the time to remove her protective clothing completely. Since I had stripped her of her underwear, she had been even more careful not to do anything that might arouse my displeasure.

When my wrist brushed her breasts, as if by chance, she inhaled sharply. Her cheeks turned red as heat shot into her skin, and because she was wearing a braid she couldn't hide her reaction.

"You're late," I said, expecting an explanation.

"It took me longer than usual to change," she mumbled, and I knew immediately what she meant. I pulled her panties out of my pocket and held them up like a trophy.

"Nolan!" She shrieked in panic, looking all around to make sure no one was watching us.

"Nobody is paying any attention to us," I replied, putting the panties back in my pocket. "Have you been thinking about me?"

"You know the answer," she replied, trying to remain calm but barely managing to look me in the eye.

Shit. Of course I'd noticed how she struggled for composure throughout the meeting, knowing that she was demonizing me for it, because I kept finding reasons to push her around.

She had no idea what she was doing to me with her innocent ways, and I hoped the allure would be over when she finally signed the contract. After one night with her, all the chaos she was causing would be over, and we could both get on with our jobs.

At that thought, I ignored the part of me that wanted to possess her. She wouldn't be my first sub, but never before had the thought of owning someone appealed to me as much as it did with Blossom.

"Of course I know the answer. I still want to hear it from you," I said, looking at her darkly.

"Yes, I was thinking about you," she finally admitted meekly.

"Good girl." I adjusted her chair.

"You can be a real gentleman when you want to," she said in surprise as she sat down.

"I'm a gentleman all the time," I replied dryly.

She gave a light giggle. "And I would have thought you had even less of a sense of humor."

"I mean it." I leaned down so that my lips grazed her earlobe. "If I wasn't a gentleman, and couldn't control myself, I would have fucked you long ago."

Her laughter caught in her throat and she cleared her throat indignantly. When I sat down, she didn't dare look me in the eye, and when the waitress brought the menu, she gratefully hid behind it.

As usual, I ordered a black coffee and a sandwich, while Blossom flicked indecisively through the menu to create further distance between us.

"A turkey sandwich with extra special sauce," she finally requested.

"She'll have the sandwich without the sauce," I corrected. She gave me an annoyed look. If she ever made it into my playroom, she was in for a treat.

"I'll have the sauce," she said firmly to the waitress, who realized that she had landed in the middle of a feud.

"Suit yourself." Shrugging, I handed back the menu, which I knew by heart. When the waitress disappeared, Blossom leaned forward.

"Stop making decisions over my head. I can decide for myself how much sauce I want on my sandwich." To reinforce her point, she gave an audible snort. It was only my stern look that reminded her that I was her boss, and that there was a power imbalance between us, even without a special contract, that she had better take into account.

"I have never doubted your independence, and I never will," I said slowly. I wasn't a bully, and I took no pleasure in forcing women into submission. If I dominated a woman, it was because she wanted it at least as much as I did—and Blossom was undoubtedly one of those women, no matter how much she denied it.

"Then why did you interfere?" she asked reproachfully, letting her gaze wander over the full tables.

"Because the sandwiches here already have too much sauce, even without the special sauce," I explained. I had been a regular for years, and knew how things worked here.

"Poor excuse," she said through clenched jaws.

"Whatever you say."

I pulled my phone out of my pocket and waited with satisfaction for the waitress to return with our drinks.

Blossom accepted her Coke and took a big gulp, while I swirled my water listlessly in its glass before putting it down again.

"No wine?" she asked curiously.

"No."

"I just thought, because you always drink a bourbon in the morning..."

"I don't drink at work," I replied. I tried to hide the tension in my voice but failed, which made Blossom flinch. "Do you?"

"No, of course not." She waved her hands emphatically. "Well, at least not at this job. At the Royal Red, Ruby makes me the best cocktails in the world."

"How did you get a job at that shack in the first place?"

"It's not a shack, it's a hidden gem," she corrected me, making no secret of the fact that I'd tinged her pride. "And Vince responded to my online resume. One thing led to another, and now I play there almost every night. Even though the journey from Queensbridge to Upper Manhattan takes forever, even when it isn't rush hour."

My ears perked up. "You live in Queensbridge?"

Even though I grew up in New York and had lived here my whole life, there were neighborhoods I avoided. If you grew up in Hell's Kitchen, you knew there were corners that were even worse. And because I had no intention of reliving old childhood memories, I preferred to stay in the better neighborhoods of the city.

"Yep. My apartment isn't exactly the Royal Renaissance Hotel, but I like it." She cocked her head to one side and looked at me questioningly as my expression hardened.

"Girls like you shouldn't live in that kind of neighborhood," I grumbled.

"Then where should I live?" she asked, displaying a naivety that made me gulp.

With me. She should fucking live with me, where I could keep an eye on her, because I was developing an unhealthy obsession, even though I felt nothing for her. Nothing. Nothing at all. And certainly no emotions.

"Somewhere where the crime rate is lower." I didn't have exact statistics in my head, but I didn't need them to know that Blossom's innocent nature would attract every guy, criminal or not.

"In that case, I'd have to drive all the way to Merryville, Texas. The whole of New York is a hotspot for crime," she answered me calmly.

"Because neighborhoods like Queensbridge make the statistics skyrocket to dizzying heights," I countered, leaving no doubt as to what I thought of the area.

She shook her head. "Don't worry, the people there are okay. Statistics or not, nothing has ever happened to me or my neighbors. I've only seen gunshots on TV, and the only addictive drug I know comes in a Ben & Jerry's carton."

I narrowed my eyes, not believing a word she said. "You'll text me when you're safely back at your apartment. Every evening. Without exception."

"Good joke." Blossom grinned wryly at me, but I remained serious.

"We've already established that I don't have a sense of humor."

Before she could say anything back, the waitress brought our order.

While I was able to eat my pastrami sandwich without any problems, Blossom got to fight with the extra sauce that had soaked the entire toast.

"Don't say it," she mumbled resignedly as she threw the dripping bread back onto the plate and looked at me with wide eyes.

"What don't you want me to say?" I bit into my sandwich as if I didn't know what she was talking about.

"That you were right and I was wrong," she said with a tone of feigned indifference that indicated she actually did care quite a bit.

"I would never allow myself to do that."

"You enjoy it, whether you want to admit it or not," she said.

I nodded, because it was true. "Yes, I enjoy it. And I won't rub your nose in it, because I'm a gentleman." I enjoyed making her regret her behavior more than I should have, because her cheeks took on a pink hue that made her even cuter than she already was.

"Thank you," she said, nodding appreciatively.

She picked up the sandwich again and took a bite. Some sauce dripped onto her wrist and she reflexively licked it off. Fuck. The way her tongue slid over her skin made me want to do unspeakable things to her.

"No more special sauce," I murmured, fighting for control with every fiber of my body as another drop of sauce landed on the underside of her arm.

"Sometimes I may not appear to be, but I'm capable of learning, boss," she said, doing the exact opposite of what she had said.

After another minute, I couldn't take it any longer.

"I'm going back to the office." I threw my sandwich back on the plate. Blossom began to get up, but I waved her off. "You're off duty, I don't need you anymore today."

I got up, threw fifty dollars on the table, and left the store before I was no longer the gentleman that she and the rest of the world thought I was.

Chapter Ten: My Life is a Taylor Swift Song

Blossom

When I entered my apartment, Little Miss Scratchy immediately padded to the entrance to wind around my legs. My heart soared because she was well again, and I picked her up to take her in my arms, which she responded to with a soft purr.

With a sweeping motion, I kicked my heels off my feet and threw my head back with a groan. Although these shoes emphasized my legs, the price was swollen ankles. I put my kitten down and went into the kitchen, which consisted of a sink and a microwave that I had scored at a pawn shop.

I filled up Miss Scratchy's bowl and she immediately dove in.

"My evening was excellent, I'm glad you asked, Miss Scratchy," I said, because I always talked to her. She wasn't the best conversationalist, but she was a good listener.

I was digging an instant burrito out of the fridge and stuffing it into the microwave when the buzzing of my phone alerted me to a message.

NOLAN: You owe me a text

"Wow," I muttered, because I hadn't expected him to be serious about the text message thing. Especially after his exit earlier. I still had no idea what had gotten into him, or if I was to blame for his behavior, but I knew one thing: if he kept treating me like that, I couldn't work for him. Debts or not, I was just too sensitive for that.

I was sorting through my thoughts, trying to figure out how to explain the details to my cat, who wasn't interested in me or my words at all, when my phone rang. My heart skipped a beat, immediately thinking it was Nolan. So even though I didn't want to admit it, I was disappointed when I saw that it was Ruby.

"Oh, it's just you," I mumbled.

"It's just me? You've never greeted me more charmingly. Who were you expecting?" she asked curiously.

"Not important," I said with a sigh. "I'm just busy at the moment."

I took the burrito out of the microwave and sat down on the couch with it.

"Let me guess: you were having a deep discussion with your cat." There was amusement in her voice. She loved Miss Scratchy dearly, so I didn't blame her for making fun of me and my cat conversations.

"Yep, we were just having a very serious conversation," I replied dryly.

"And that's totally normal, and not at all worrying," Ruby said, her tone dripping with sarcasm.

"Exactly. It's perfectly normal, and nothing to worry about," I replied, as if I hadn't heard her cynicism. "What's up?"

She and I had recently spoken at the Royal Red, so I was all the more curious to hear what else she had to tell me.

"Nothing, really." Her voice was an octave higher than normal. In general, she had no talent for feigning interest or disinterest.

"If you're going to start like that..." I began, but left the end of the sentence open.

"What do you mean?" she asked, sounding miffed. I heard a beer bottle pop open in the background.

"Last time, when there was 'really nothing' to call you about, I had to drive across New York in the middle of the night to rescue you from the worst date ever. You know, the guy who..."

"Yes! I didn't forget!" she cut me off so I wouldn't keep talking.

I began to giggle. "Oh come on, there's nothing wrong with men having a hobby." My laughter echoed through the apartment, and Miss Scratchy gave me a confused look.

"I wouldn't call it a hobby, more of a morbid obsession," Ruby replied bitterly.

"What, just because he was a *Lord of the Rings* fan?" My stomach hurt from laughing, but I couldn't stop.

"I have nothing against a wall poster, or even one of those super-expensive special collector's DVD boxes, if you like. But there are some things that go too far." Ruby was still upset about the outcome of their date, and I shouldn't tease her about it anymore, but it had just been too crazy to be true. "He was really hot, but when he busted out the elf ears and hobbit feet, I just had to bail. Just like any normal person would have done. Actually, I should have been suspicious when he asked about my ring size."

"Oh, don't take it so seriously, it could have been much worse," I said, trying not to have another fit of laughter.

"Name one person who is worse," she insisted. I could see her in my imagination, tilting her head and putting one hand on her hip.

"My boss, for example," I blurted. Startled, I put my hand over my mouth, regretting my spontaneous words.

"I'm glad you brought that up, that's the real reason I'm calling."

What a bummer. I had suspected that, but it was too late to get out of the phone call now.

"Why? Do you want me to arrange a date with him?" I teased, hoping she was just interested in his looks. There was no question that she and Vince had Googled him by now.

"If he's as hot as you say, maybe," Ruby replied. I could tell she was almost bursting, because she knew exactly how attractive Nolan Caldwell was. Even without the power he had, and the billions in his bank account, women would fall at his feet in droves.

At least until he treated them as coldly as he treated me.

"I would strongly advise against it," I advised her, because I doubted that Mr. Icecold was capable of a relationship.

"Because you want him for yourself? No problem, sister, I don't begrudge you a good match." I tried to detect irony or sarcasm in her voice, but she was serious.

"What? No!" I protested so loudly that my credibility suffered. But I was completely sincere. "Why do you even want to talk about Nolan?"

"Nolan? So you're already on first name terms with him," she said. I could hear the grin in her voice. "I just wanted to know if everything was okay at your job, because you haven't said anything about it yet. But we can skip the boring stuff and get straight to the point where I help you wrap him around your finger."

"I'd rather jump back to the point about it being my *job*, and everything is going fine," I said, even though I'd been busy all evening trying not to talk about my new job at Caldwell Industries. Just the thought of Nolan still owning my panties made me dizzy.

"Come on, do I have to pull everything out of your nose? I need more details."

"There's nothing else to report because it's a completely normal job."

Luckily, Ruby couldn't see how red my cheeks were getting, because I was lying through my teeth. But I just couldn't talk about how insane Nolan was driving me with his ambivalent behavior. On the one hand, he made no secret of how unhappy he was with me, but at the same time he made me feel like he wanted me. And the worst thing about it was that I wasn't averse to it. On the contrary, the only thing holding me back was the fear that I was too inexperienced for him.

"No problems?" Ruby pressed.

"It's going as you'd expect." With a shrug, I took a bite of my burrito, which was now cold, but which I had completely forgotten about during the conversation.

"Could you get any more cryptic than that?"

I loved my best friend, but I hated her dogged curiosity when it came to my love life. My non-existent love life, mind you.

"You know he only gave me the job so that he could make sure I paid him back," I explained with a sigh, because she wouldn't shut up otherwise.

"These are the best conditions for a love story!" My friend wasn't a romantic, so I was all the more surprised by her words.

"I guess my life is more like a Taylor Swift song," I replied ironically. "I think he really hates me because I scratched his car."

No matter what I thought was going on between him and I, that stupid scratch would come between us forever, that much was clear. Ruby began to say something back, but all of a sudden I heard someone banging enthusiastically on my door.

"Are you expecting visitors?" she asked in surprise, because the knocking was so loud that she could hear it through the phone.

"No," I replied in confusion, jumping up from the couch and peering through the peephole. The blood drained from my face. "Oh God."

"Blossom, this is not a good situation to say something like 'oh God', because then I think there's a crazed ax murderer with a thirst for blood at the door!"

"Not a crazy ax murderer," I whispered. I continued to stare at the man standing on the other side of my door with an angry expression.

"I have to go, my boss is at the door."

Chapter Eleven: Sign it, Little Dove

Blossom

Nolan Caldwell knocked firmly on the door once more. My heart was pounding in my throat.

What in God's name was he doing here?

"Either you open the door, or I'll kick it in," he called through the door. I had no doubt that he would make good on his threat.

I opened the door and he invited himself into my apartment. I bit my lip so as not to say anything I might regret, because I had a dozen curses on the tip of my tongue. After all, he was still my boss, to whom I was indebted and on whose salary I depended.

His dark gaze traveled down my spine and sent a shiver down my spine.

"You're wearing that dress again," he said snidely. He had made it his mission to insult this dress until I hated it too.

"I had to work," I explained as I smoothed out the red silk fabric.

"You work for me. And I thought I made myself clear," he replied in a deadpan tone, sending another shiver down my spine. Another sign that I had terrible taste in men, because part of me secretly liked that he was pulling this Mr. Icecold shtick, and yet seemed interested in me at the same time.

"But I also work for Vince, and I will continue to work for him. I haven't had time to get another dress yet." I tried to put my hands on my hips confidently, but because authority didn't look good on me, I looked awkward rather than self-assured, so I let my arms hang at my sides again.

"We'll talk about that later," he said, leaving me in no doubt that we really did have a bone to pick with each other. Why did I like it so much? I shouldn't be playing this game, especially because I didn't know the rules. But I wanted to anyway, because I knew that something like this would never happen to me again.

"What are you doing here?" I asked, because he hadn't said anything about his reason for visiting yet.

"Making sure you're okay," he replied, crossing his arms in front of his chest. His answer made me blink in confusion, because his concern seemed almost genuine.

"I'm fine." I held the door open, waiting for him to take the hint to leave. But he didn't move an inch, just stared at me angrily.

"You didn't respond," he growled, pulling his phone out of his pocket.

"I thought it was a joke," I replied with a shrug. Joke was probably the wrong word, but I'd been sure he was putting me down because he thought my neighborhood was the worst crime hole in New York.

Yes, the neighborhood wasn't very fancy, but in my eyes it wasn't as unsafe as he made it out to be.

"And the messages I wrote to you were also a joke? If you think you see me laughing, you're wrong." He took a step toward me and our height difference became even more obvious. I barely reached his neck, even when I stood on tiptoe.

"You texted me again?" I asked, confused. Instinctively, I tightened my grip on my phone, but I couldn't take my eyes off him to see if he had really written.

"Don't act so innocent," he snapped, making no secret of the fact that he thought I was somehow trying to manipulate him.

At least once he knew me longer, he would realize that I only lied in response to one thing:

Yes, I'm fine. That sentence was almost always a lie, one that had lost all meaning for me, but kept those around me calm, and meant that no one would bombard me with even more painful questions.

Totally fine.

Little Miss Scratchy, who usually fled under the bed when visitors came, came up to Nolan as if it were the most normal thing in the world and wrapped herself around his leg.

Lousy traitor. What surprised me even more than my cat's behavior was Nolan's reaction to it. He knelt down and scratched her favorite spot behind her ear until she contentedly hopped onto the sofa and curled up. I had thought he was many things, but not a cat person. Or an animal person in general. Or someone who could demonstrate anything other than hatred and contempt for others.

"I saw you sent me a text," I finally conceded when he gave me a demanding look.

"Look at your phone." He put his phone back and kept his hand in his pocket. He was really good at issuing orders you couldn't refuse, because he made you feel like it was right.

I obeyed and unlocked my phone.

NOLAN: Write to me.

NOLAN: Now.

NOLAN: I'm waiting, little dove.

NOLAN: Do I have to come over?

"Oh..." I said, smiling awkwardly at him because I had missed his messages.

"Is that all you have to say?" He raised his left eyebrow and looked at me reprovingly. Making me feel guilty was another thing he was really good at.

"What do you want to hear from me?" I asked, because I really didn't know what he wanted from me now. "No matter what I say or do, it won't change the fact that you hate me."

There. I had said what I felt, even if it was possibly unwise. Nolan was unpredictable, after all, and his actions never ceased to amaze me, just like his eyes did now.

"I don't hate you," he replied coolly but sincerely.

"Then what happened at the restaurant at lunchtime today? When you just left me like that?" I asked. His quick exit had really hurt me and there was no doubt in my mind that it had been because of me.

"I had my reasons." He took another step closer. So close that I could smell his perfume. Sandalwood blended with the bourbon taste of his lips; it acted like an aphrodisiac on me.

"You may have had your reasons, but I don't understand them because you don't explain them to me," I replied thoughtfully. It seemed to me that Nolan was even better at hiding his true feelings than I was.

"Reasons you don't need to know."

Anger boiled up inside me, because his answer was a non-answer. It got me nowhere, especially not closer to him.

"Is it still about your car?" I asked. I hadn't been working at Caldwell Tower long, but everyone I'd told my employment story to had turned white as a sheet from the moment I mentioned the car paint. But I couldn't quite believe that Nolan had any more feelings for that pile of metal than he did for his fellow man, no matter how unhealthy my own relationship with cars was.

The anger that flashed in his eyes said everything I needed to know. For reasons I didn't understand, he really resented me for the damage, even though I was doing everything I could to make amends. I would pay the debt, but even if I hadn't been able to pay, the repair cost to him would have been peanuts, or rather peanut crumbs. The crumbs of the crumbs of his peanut crumbs.

"You should go now." I opened the door a crack wider to make my demand clear. "And when my debt to you is paid, I'll leave and not bother you again."

His eyes narrowed as he walked toward me. At first I thought he was really going to disappear from my apartment, but I was wrong. He shut the door and pushed me so far back that I bumped my back against the closed door.

"You should have responded to me." His voice was a deep growl that reminded me of a hungry wolf. My heart was racing, because he was looking at me like he had in the elevator when he stole my panties. Under no circumstances could I show him how much I enjoyed that kind of attention, because it would get me in hot water... or in his bed, which was even worse.

"I thought you were joking," I continued to defend myself. How could I have known that he was serious, as aloof and disinterested as he was most of the time?

"I never make jokes. Or do you see me laughing? You should know what makes me tick by now."

"Now I know." I inhaled sharply as his body pressed even tighter against me. "Why do you even care if I've arrived home?"

His eyes darkened, and I could see him searching for words. He was trying to hide his feelings, but his icy wall crumbled and emotions came out that he couldn't deny.

"I'm... interested in you," he replied.

The truth in his words overwhelmed me. "Why?" My question was no more than a whisper, but he understood me anyway.

"If I knew..." He looked at me questioningly, as if I had an answer, but I was just as much in the dark as he was. I knew exactly what he meant. There was something between us that no one could describe or understand, but it was there. And neither of us wanted to admit it.

"Why are you here?" I continued to ask. "You could have called, or sent someone else."

"I'm here because I'm not used to being contradicted, or worse, ignored."

I believed him immediately. His engaging manner and determination could be overwhelming. He had reached the top of the corporate ladder, there was no higher to go, and everyone knew that it took more than just good business sense.

"And what are you going to do about it?" I continued. I shouldn't have asked, but I needed to hear his answer. I wanted to find out how far we could take this game. If I had to describe it, I would have said I was out of control, for the first time in a long time, and it felt damn good.

"Sign the contract," he whispered in my ear.

I inhaled sharply. "I wish I could," I replied with a sigh. Under other circumstances, I would have signed the contract long ago.

"What's stopping you?" he asked, searching my face for the answer.

"I'm scared." I had to tell him the truth, but it wasn't easy for me.

"Of what?" he asked.

"That I will disappoint you." I tried to push him away from me, but his body was too strong. He didn't move an inch. "I just can't take any more hate."

"Again, little dove, I don't hate you." He stroked a strand of hair out of my face and there was a tingle where his thumb touched my cheek.

"I've never signed a contract like this before," I continued. My whole body was throbbing, and the taste of bourbon on his lips, so close to mine, made me weak.

"Sign, little dove." His tongue traveled down my neck. There was no better argument.

"That's unfair," I whispered back. How could I resist him? "You leave me no choice but to sign."

"Right." He grinned devilishly at me.

"How does it work then?" I asked, hoping that he would say something that would make me refuse. Because so far his arguments were good enough that I barely had the strength to resist him. Normally I wasn't so quick to let people get to me, especially men with more self-confidence than was good for them, but Nolan was an exception for reasons unknown to me.

"I'll show you what a bad girl you've been, so that you won't throw my warnings and orders to the wind in future. And I'll make sure you're a better girl in the future. My girl." His promising words made my whole body tingle.

"If I sign, am I your girl?" I asked, which elicited a growl from him.

"My little dove. My girl. Mine."

Those words finished me off.

"I'll sign," I replied, breathing heavily. I might regret my decision later because it screamed heartbreak, but my gut also told me that I would never regret this night, no matter what happened in the future.

Nolan may not have been my dream prince in gold armor, riding up to me on a white horse, but he was the first man to make my heart beat faster, and do things to my head that were inexplicable to me. Hopefully my virginity really wasn't a problem for him. Not that I cared, it was just that the opportunity to get rid of it had never presented itself. Until now. And now, I was getting ready to get rid of it so fast it was making me dizzy.

He pulled an envelope and a pen from the inside of his jacket and handed them to me. My rapid heartbeat pounded in my ears as I read through the papers and signed them.

My God, I had really done it. I had signed Nolan's contract and now I was his.

"Your safeword," he said when he saw the blank space on the contract that I had deliberately left out.

"Will I need one?" I asked, frowning.

He looked at me without answering, so I pressed, "Has anyone ever needed a safeword with you?" There was no question that he had handed out contracts before me. But I didn't want to think about it too long because I wanted to maintain the illusion that he was really interested in me. For me, not just for my flesh.

"No." He looked at me calmly without making a face. Whatever he did, he knew exactly what effect it had on me.

"How many women have broken or terminated the contract?" I continued. He was so close to me that I found it difficult to put my thoughts into words.

"None." He rested his hand on the door behind me and I gasped. He was starting to get impatient, but he made no move to stop me.

"And how many times have you broken or terminated the contract?" That was my last question, which I thought I already knew the answer to.

"All of them. I've canceled every single contract."

That was exactly what I had feared. He was a heartbreaker, and I had to be careful not to become his next victim. But I just couldn't refuse any longer. I no longer had the strength to resist the attraction he was exuding.

"I don't need a safeword," I said firmly.

"That could be dangerous for you, little dove." His free hand stroked my cheek.

"I trust you," I replied. It was the truth. The fact that he had stormed my apartment in the middle of the night proved to me that Nolan wanted to, and could, look after me.

"You should be careful what feelings you express to me," he urged after thinking about my words.

"Then you'd better be careful what feelings you trigger in me," I replied with the same sharpness. We both had to be careful what feelings we had for each other.

"You have no idea what feelings you're triggering in me right now," he whispered in my ear.

"Enlighten me." I looked at him expectantly, because I wanted to know what was going on inside him. I wanted to understand Nolan better, and hoped that he would let me, because I couldn't deal with the indifference he so often threw at me.

"It's better if I don't let you look into my abyss." He took the contract and put it back in his jacket. "Tomorrow in the office, you tell me your safeword. I can't take you to your limits without a safety leash."

"Okay."

"Okay, *sir*," he corrected me. It was in the contract, but to be honest, I had blocked out everything I had read there. I could barely manage to stand still, how was I supposed to think about contractual rules?

"Yes, sir." After I answered, he pressed me against the door and kissed me hard.

"You have no idea how long I've waited for this," he whispered against my lips.

"It was just one day," I replied.

"It was half a fucking eternity." He kissed me again. This time he didn't stop before my whole body shook and I felt dizzy.

"Fuck," he murmured quietly. "I really hate this dress."

He slipped it over my shoulders, and as it slipped down my arms, I gasped in panic and held the fabric of the dress tightly. I didn't want him to see the scars that I hid, not only from the world, but also from myself, because they reminded me every time of that one night that I so desperately wanted to forget.

When he noticed my panic, he paused and gazed at me thoughtfully.

"You said you trusted me, little dove. Now you can prove it."

He was giving me a way out, and I was grateful to him for that, but he was right. Trust was worth nothing if you didn't test it. So I slowly took off the dress and let it fall to the floor.

I watched Nolan's every expression as he saw my scarred arm. Over the years, most of the incisions had faded but were still clearly visible.

Ironically, the surgical scars were barely visible, but they were by far the ones that hurt the most, because the wounds had reached into my soul.

"Did you do this to yourself?" he asked seriously.

"No." I shook my head and his gaze darkened. His jaws ground tightly together and hatred flared in his eyes that I had seen before.

"Then who did, and where can I find him?" he continued. His eyes took on an expression that took my breath away. Wild, unbridled rage, together with boundless hatred flickered in them.

"It was an accident," I answered hastily. It wasn't a lie, but it wasn't the whole truth either, because I just couldn't bring myself to talk about it. "A car accident."

"You don't like talking about it." That wasn't a question, but a statement, which I answered with a nod. "Then we'll talk about other things now."

"Thank you," I whispered, barely audibly, exhaling with relief because he finally knew the reason for my strange behavior.

He took my hand and led me to the bed, which was only separated from the rest of the room by a screen. When he saw the candles on my bedside table, which I never lit because I lived with an unpredictable cat, he smiled.

"Let's talk about the fact that you've been a pretty bad girl for wearing panties again. Or better yet, I'll talk while you listen and don't make another sound."

"I'm good at that," I replied and immediately received a stern look. "From now on."

In front of the bed, Nolan took off my panties, then lit one of the candles. I hadn't thought he was a romantic, but in the last few minutes he had turned my entire world view upside down, so a few lit candles didn't change anything.

He stared at my entire body, his expression one that any woman would kill for.

"You're perfect," he said, so convincingly that I had to believe him. He thought I was perfect, and I wanted to burst into tears because he really made me feel perfect. Completely. No one had ever done that before him. Not Vince, not Ruby, not Rhyan, and certainly not my family.

He gently pushed me down so that I had to lie back on the bed. When his hand moved along my stomach, I reared up again.

"Nolan, I have to…" I began, because I shouldn't keep the virginity issue quiet, but he interrupted me.

"All you're going to do is keep quiet, keep still, and enjoy." He placed my wrists next to my head. "I should warn you, little dove. I am an epicure. Every time you move, I will wait longer as you writhe beneath me, craving more, begging for an orgasm. But your orgasms are mine, and I will only give them to you when you have earned them. So be a good girl and let me dominate you."

I leaned back and obeyed, which was quite easy for me with the way he was touching me. His hands slid over my body and touched points that made me moan. I had often imagined myself losing my virginity, but it had never involved a dominant man and so many feelings. On the contrary, just one of Nolan's touches made all my fantasies fade away.

When he took a nipple between his thumb and forefinger, then the other, I drew in a sharp breath. They became more and more sensitive under his touch and I barely managed to stay still. My whole body fought against it. This mixture of pain and arousal alone almost made me come and my body screamed louder and louder for release.

I wanted him. I wanted him so badly that I found it hard not to rip the clothes off his body and beg him to finally take me.

He took the lit candle from the bedside table and dripped some wax on his wrist. Then he grinned maliciously at me when I realized that he was anything but a romantic, and had other plans for the candle.

The first drop hit my stomach and made me gasp because it had caught me completely unaware. I saw the next drop before it landed, but the pain remained the same. More and more wax dripped on my body and the heat inside me continued to rise.

I began to whimper as he hit the sensitive skin of the underside of my upper arms, not missing a single spot. And when I thought I already knew the most intense pain the candle could cause, the first drops on my nipples catapulted me into unknown spheres. Pain exploded in my body, along with a deep desire that I couldn't describe.

Because I wanted to rear up as another gush of wax hit my breasts, Nolan pushed me back onto the bed with one hand.

"Hold still, little dove," he urged me. I nodded, but also gave him a pleading look, hoping that he would finally give me what I wanted. However, his answering gaze told me that he had other plans for me, and I hated him for it. Ever since he kissed me, he had always managed to awaken feelings in me that I had never known, and some of them felt so good that I was already afraid that I would never be able to feel them again if Nolan and I went our separate ways.

Because there was no question that it would end like this. How long would it last? He was my boss. My hellishly attractive but unapproachable boss. Our worlds were too different to fit together. He loved cars; I not only hated them, I was afraid of them. He was richer than Midas, whereas I had more overdrafts than degrees. But the main difference between the two of us was that Nolan knew exactly where he wanted to be in life, whereas I was stumbling from day to day, hoping to get by somehow.

As wax dripped down to my core I was really close to an orgasm. My breathing was rapid and my eyelids fluttered as I threw my head back and enjoyed the tingling sensation that flooded my entire body.

"Don't come," he murmured. "Don't forget that your orgasms are mine."

I bit my lips to keep from protesting; as a reward, his hand slipped between my legs. He rubbed my pearl and I moaned with relief because he was finally touching me the way I had wanted all along.

Nolan growled softly as he felt how ready I was for him. His fingers had already burned a mark into my skin. Without a doubt, he would stay in my memory forever, no matter what else happened in my life. I hoped that this first time was truly memorable and would stay with me forever. And at the same time, I was afraid that no man would ever come close to what he did to me.

He massaged my most sensitive spot with circular movements until he finally unbuttoned his shirt and opened his pants.

I had already guessed how muscular he was under his suit, but his toned body surpassed all my fantasies. His smooth skin stretched tightly over his six-pack, which ended in a "V" that would drive half the women's world crazy. He didn't have an ounce of fat on his flawless body. When did he have time to work out so much?

He slipped off his pants and I held my breath when I saw how big he was. Too big for me, definitely!

He bent down on the bed and pushed my legs apart. When I made a move to touch his body, he grabbed my wrists and fixed them next to my head.

"Don't move, little dove," he whispered reprovingly. Our bodies were almost touching and it was driving me crazy. I wanted to touch him, bury my fingers in his perfect hairstyle and run my fingers along the contours of his six-pack. And the longer he denied me, the hotter the desire burned.

He rubbed his hardness between my legs, massaged me further, and almost brought me to climax.

"Relax," he whispered in my ear as he felt me tense up beneath him. I wanted him, I wanted him badly, but I was also unsure because I didn't know how his manhood would fit inside me.

"I don't know if it will fit," I whispered.

Nolan smiled at me. "It will be fine, Blossom. Because that's exactly what your body has been signaling to me all along."

"But I..." I wanted to protest again, but he put a finger to my lips.

"You trust me and that's good. It's the basis of what we do here. But you also have to trust yourself."

I nodded because he was right. My insecurities had stood in my way long enough, now it was time to leave them behind.

"I won't take you to the limit until you give me your safeword," he said, looking at me seriously. My whole body shook and suddenly I wanted him to take me to my limits and beyond.

"Florida!" I blurted out. "Florida is my safe word."

"Good girl." He stroked my hair and I enjoyed the tenderness he showed me because it happened so rarely. "Relax."

He rubbed his tip against my entrance and I held my breath as he entered me with a single thrust. Jesus Christ. It took a moment for me to get used to his size and Nolan gave me that time. After the panic of the unknown subsided, all that was left was an unfamiliar feeling that disappeared once he started to move.

To be honest, I was still stunned that I could take it in, but it felt intoxicating and I wanted more.

"You really can be a good girl," he whispered. And I smiled at him. The Nolan who had just taken me was completely different to the one I had to work for. He was literally a sight for sore eyes.

The faster he moved, the more my body trembled as so many sensations flowed through me that I felt dizzy. When he realized that I was getting closer and closer to my orgasm, he thrust even harder without giving me permission to come. I still thought he was a real turn-on, but he was also a rotten bastard who I hated.

Only when my moans turned into whimpers did he look at me with a mild expression.

"Keep being my good girl and come for me," he whispered.

I exploded. Black dots flashed before my eyes, I was hot and cold at the same time and every fiber of my body was tingling.

I pulled myself tightly around him and when I came to properly, I noticed that he didn't stop but kept going. He kept fucking me until I saw stars again and I enjoyed it. Nolan hadn't made empty promises when he said he wanted to push me to my limits.

"Please," I begged quietly.

"Is it too much for you, little dove?" he asked, without changing the tempo or intensity of his thrusts. I shook my head.

"I want more," I replied, which made him smile. He should smile more often...

"You're pretty brave to demand something from me, even though you know where your place is," he replied.

"Please," I continued to whisper without admitting my mistake.

"You wouldn't have it any other way, little dove."

With a single movement, he grabbed my hips and turned me onto my stomach before penetrating me again. At this angle, he was able to take me even deeper and I screamed every time he sank deep inside me.

He took me even harder than the first time and I loved how tightly he gripped my hips so that he could thrust even deeper. I bent down further, put my head to one side and dug my nails into the sheet, which smelled of him by now.

The next orgasm came over me so unexpectedly that it took me by surprise. But that didn't mean I didn't enjoy it. On the contrary, I welcomed the burning in my veins and didn't care if Nolan gave me a reprimanding look for coming without his permission.

The second time, it took even longer for me to come back to reality. I sank down further, but his grip remained tenacious.

"I don't think I can take any more," I gasped breathlessly.

"Are you finished?" His hand traveled along my spine.

I nodded. "Yes."

"You came without my permission. And until I make it clear to you that there are consequences for disobeying my orders, I will not stop."

Oh God. Breathless, I continued to let him take me and it was the most exciting thing that had ever happened to me. The third orgasm was approaching and I wondered if it was normal to come so often the first time. Nolan knew exactly what to do to trigger these crazy feelings in me and I hated and loved him for it in equal measure.

Only after I had really reached my limit did he allow me one last orgasm before he came himself.

When he pulled out of me and saw the bloodstains, his eyes darkened.

"Don't tell me you were a virgin." Judging by the look on his face, the question was rhetorical, which is why I kept quiet.

"Blossom," he growled. "Answer me."

"I'm not supposed to say I was a virgin, so I can't answer anything, sir." I tilted my head without taking my eyes off him. I found it difficult to interpret his expression.

"Fuck." He looked me up and down as if checking to see if I was still whole. I was no longer whole, I was now complete.

"You should have said something," he said calmly, but his hands were still clenched into fists.

"I could have said something, yes. But I didn't want to," I replied, shrugging my shoulders.

"Why? I would have dealt with you differently."

"Exactly," I argued. I had secretly liked his rough treatment even more than I admitted. "Besides, I deserve my punishment."

Now his fixed expression gave way to a grin.

"There's more to you than I expected, little dove."

"Thank you." I smiled at him, then slid sideways on my bed to make room for him. But Nolan Caldwell was no romantic and I should have realized that.

"The fact that we've been busy for so long is no excuse for you not to be in the office on time tomorrow. And I expect you not to wear underwear," he said dryly. "Lock the door behind me."

Then he got up and got dressed, leaving me exhausted and with the craziest feelings in the world, alone in my apartment.

Chapter Twelve: What You Want and What You Need can be Worlds Apart, Little Dove

Nolan

"You're on time," I said without looking up as Blossom put a coffee on my desk at seven o'clock sharp.

"You seem surprised," she replied with a smile.

"I am surprised." I looked her up and down. She tried not to let on that I had ravaged her last night, but she failed. I knew for a fact that she could still feel me every step of the way. It left me with ambivalent feelings that I had taken her virginity.

Maybe I was a bad person, but I loved the thought that I had burned myself into her memory forever. No girl forgets her first time, which meant Blossom would never forget me.

"Was your punishment not severe enough?" I asked. A blush immediately rose in her cheeks and she gasped for air.

"Yes, sir, the message has arrived." She nodded several times and cleared her throat. "All the messages. Even the one about punctuality."

I knew from her shining eyes what words she was expecting from me now.

"Good girl." I drank my bourbon, then stood up and stood in front of her so that she was trapped between me and the desk. I liked the effect my gestures had on her, and how clearly she reacted to them. One look was enough to make her hold her breath. With a touch, I was able to make it clear that I knew exactly what I was doing to her.

I pressed her against the desk and slipped my hand under her skirt. When I felt the hem of her panties, I growled.

"Didn't I tell you not to wear underwear?" I asked, trying to control myself. I hated it when my orders were disobeyed, and it took all my strength not to rip her clothes off. I didn't usually have a problem with torn fabric, unless it involved Blossom. She was stubborn, and perhaps a little naive, refusing to wear clothes that wouldn't drive the men's world crazy.

"I guess you don't have another evening dress either?" I asked with a cynical tone.

She looked at me in surprise. "I thought…"

"Yes? What did you think, little dove?" I brushed a strand of hair out of her face and waited for her answer. My exterior remained calm, but inside I was seething.

"I thought that was just foreplay. So, afterward, I didn't take it seriously." Her voice was no more than a whisper, lending her words more innocence than I could stomach.

"Did you lock your door?" I pressed.

"Of course." She frowned, looking at me as if I had lost my mind for asking.

"So you did take me seriously after all, you just ignored part of it," I stated matter-of-factly, and she had to nod in agreement.

I held out my hand. "Give me those."

"You're really serious," she said in astonishment. At the same time, her breath quickened and she unconsciously bit her lower lip, because she liked my dominance.

"Of course. Do you think I would draw up contracts otherwise?" I asked.

She bit her lip. "I thought this was kind of a game for you, too."

My gaze darkened and she caught her breath.

"I never play," I murmured against her ear. My hand slid along her neck and I squeezed lightly. Too lightly to take her breath away, but firmly enough to show her that I meant business. She moaned under my touch, then braced herself against the desk as her knees went weak.

"You signed my contract, and I expect you to take everything it says seriously. But because you don't have any experience yet, I'll cut you some slack." Not too much. Just thinking about how I was about to punish her made me hard.

"Thank you." She tried to push herself away from the table and leave the office, but I held her tight.

"Where are you off to so quickly?" I pulled her close to me so that she could feel what she had done.

"I have to work," she replied hoarsely. Every word flowed viscously, like honey, over her lips.

"Your job is to serve me. I did not permit you to leave." I gripped her delicate wrist tighter. "Before you go, I will make it very clear to you that you had better take me seriously."

I kissed her so gently that it must have been unsatisfactory, considering my harsh words. She wanted me to kiss her with the same hardness, to fuck her, to make her senseless.

"Bend over the table," I murmured. She jerked sharply, but she was about to comply, but the office door opened and she flinched.

"Dylan. You're almost on time." I shoved my hands in my pockets and suppressed a grin as Blossom's cheeks turned a deep red. To be honest, I had forgotten about our meeting. If only he'd been a minute later...

After he came into the office, Karen followed him, giving us a meaningful look. I had no intention of hiding the fact that I was fucking Blossom. Maybe she would finally get over me.

"I'm not even going to ask where Bruce is. Let's get started." I waved Dylan over to me. Then I turned to Blossom. "Please bring me the thing we were discussing."

"That thing we were just discussing?" she echoed, her voice hoarse.

"Yes. Now. In an envelope."

"Of course, sir." She walked away with shaky steps, which was noticed by Dylan.

"You shouldn't shoo your assistant like that, or at least give her different shoes."

"It's not the shoes," I replied flatly. It was me. I was the reason why she had to think about what I had done to her last night, and what I would repeat tonight every time she took a step.

I pointed to the seat in front of me. "Let's get started."

Karen immediately placed all the documents in perfect order on the desk, and Dylan discussed the details of today's agenda. I didn't listen, but stared at the closed door until Blossom came back, her cheeks a brilliant shade of red, and handed me a brown document envelope.

When I opened it, she let out a yip that she tried to hide with a cough. Satisfied, I threw the envelope and its contents into the bottom drawer and tried to listen to Dylan at least a little.

But my thoughts kept drifting back to Blossom, who was still waiting for her punishment. I hated it when I couldn't finish things straight away. Uncharacteristically for me, I worked through things faster than normal, which Dylan commented on with a frown. He looked at Karen, who hadn't taken her eyes off us for a second.

"Karen, can you get us some coffee and sandwiches?" he asked.

"Of course. I'll tell Nolan's assistant," she said, rising to her feet.

"I want you to get them," Dylan replied quickly.

"But I..." she began.

"But nothing," Dylan interrupted her. "Pastrami, without tomatoes. And the same for Nolan. Also without tomatoes."

"With tomatoes," I corrected him, but he shook his head.

"Without tomatoes. Two orders without tomatoes doubles the chance that one of them really is without tomatoes," he explained.

I shrugged, aware of his near-fatal tomato allergy.

"Fine by me, pastrami without tomatoes." I continued to stare at my documents. "But make sure you get a few extra slices of tomato on the side."

I continued to stare stubbornly at the papers in front of me, but my concentration was failing. Normally my subs left me stone cold, but Blossom? She seemed to have nested in my thoughts, and wouldn't leave me alone for a second. She was almost as penetrating as Karen, except that my little dove was unaware of her effect on me.

Karen disappeared from my office, and as soon as she closed the door, Dylan let out a sigh.

"You have to hit her with a fence post before she'll take the hint that you want some privacy." He leaned back in his chair and crossed his arms in front of his chest.

"She understood you, she just didn't want to go," I replied dryly. Karen was a tough opportunist, and always knew what she wanted, so she was so predictable that it bored me.

"It's the same thing. And I get my revenge next time we're in the ring, buddy," Dylan said with a grin.

"She's annoying, but she does a good job." Otherwise I would have fired her long ago. But it took forever to find an assistant who understood her job and had familiarized herself with the company. Sexual opportunism or not, she was important for the merger, even if she was a pain in the ass for all of us.

"If by a good job you mean she's wearing out my nerves, which means you might finally stand a chance against me at the Haven, then yes, she's doing a damn good job." He smirked at me challengingly. "Why exactly am I not dumping her on Bruce?"

"Because Bruce would give us both hell," I replied. He had even less patience for women like Karen than we did.

"So?" Dylan furrowed his eyebrows.

"And you know exactly how long we worked to get him to agree to a merger." I leaned back and tapped on the documents.

"It's funny how he only ever sees the worst in people, but then gives us a completely free hand."

He was right. Not that Dylan or I were gullible or naive, but Bruce seemed to have had the hardest fate of all of us.

"We're an exception," I commented.

Bruce, Dylan and I had been through all kinds of shit, but our views didn't get in the way of our friendship. On the contrary, without Left Hook Haven, we'd have no anchor, no family. Our loyalty had taken a long time to develop, but now it was unbreakable.

"You're right," Dylan replied, rubbing his knuckles.

We focused on work again, and by the time Karen returned with sandwiches and coffee, we were wrapping up. Dylan rose to his feet just as Blossom entered the office with the organized stack of papers that we had just printed to record our progress.

Karen placed the sandwich bag and the paper cups on my desk, bending down so low that it was impossible not to look at her cleavage. The sight left me cold, and that's exactly what I signaled.

I took the brown envelope out of the bottom drawer and dropped it on the table.

"We have something else to talk about, Blossom."

"Yes, sir." She walked toward me uncertainly, clearly uncomfortable under Karen's gaze, even though she was the eye-catcher in every room. She shifted her weight uneasily and avoided the stares. She urgently needed to work on her self-confidence if she wanted to survive in my world.

Karen bent down even lower to thrust her surgically-enhanced breasts toward me.

"If there's anything else we need to discuss, Nolan, let me know. You can call anytime." She winked at me. "Anytime, really."

I didn't answer, but waved my hand through the air to beckon Blossom over.

"Blossom. Today."

"Right away!" She handed me the documents she had taken from the printer, and as she was about to leave, I grabbed her wrist.

"We still have something to discuss."

"I'll see you at the Haven tonight," Dylan said, heading for the door.

Karen trotted after him, but left the door open, which Blossom immediately closed when she noticed my gaze.

"The thing with the panties?" she asked.

"Exactly. Or, to call a spade a spade... obedience." I took my time answering, because the calmer I got, the more restless Blossom became. "No more panties. And no more red dress in the Royal Red."

She took a breath, presumably to protest, but I raised my finger. "Not a sound."

She bit her lip even harder and waited patiently for my next command.

"Bend over the table."

Her gaze slid to the closed door. I stood up and turned the key. "Next time I catch you in your underwear, I'll leave the door wide open. Understood?"

"Yes, sir." She nodded eagerly and leaned on my desk.

"You should still be quiet so no one hears what I do to you." I grinned lopsidedly at her and she gasped. Damn, why did I love it so much when she breathed heavily?

I stood behind her, pushed her skirt up, and let my hands glide over her soft skin. I pushed her legs apart with my hand and, as if unintentionally, grazed her wet folds. I hadn't done anything to her yet and yet she was ready for me. Fuck.

"One hundred strokes for ignoring my orders. I want you to keep count." Then I began to spank her bottom until red marks appeared on her skin. She gasped with each stroke, but bravely withstood my treatment. After one hundred spanks, her backside was at least as red as her cheeks, but I wasn't done with her yet. Her moans were just too sweet.

"I haven't heard anything. So let's start from scratch."

"That's unfair!" she blurted out, until she saw my reproachful look and cleared her throat. "I mean, yes, sir!"

I leaned down and stroked the back of her head. My lips came so close that I touched her earlobe.

"Be a good girl and endure the next hundred strokes for me too," I whispered. Blossom began to count my strokes, panting and moaning heavily.

With each stroke, my intensity increased because I simply couldn't control myself as more pleasure gathered between her legs with each stroke. After the first fifty strokes, I took a break and let my fingertips wander over her bare skin.

"You're lucky you came across me to explore what you like, little dove." I paused to let the words sink in. "I'm not a man for life. Shit, I'm not even a man for more than one date. But I know exactly what girls like you want and need."

"Isn't that the same thing?" she asked, blinking.

"What you want and what you need can sometimes be worlds apart," I replied and smiled meaningfully. Then I took the next swing and elicited heavenly sounds from her.

"If you don't want everyone to know what I'm doing to you, you'd better keep quiet," I urged her.

"It's hard when you hit so hard," she replied, panting and glaring at me with a mixture of arousal and anger.

"Did I hear that more firmly, little dove? You can have that." I doubled my intensity for the last few strokes and Blossom clawed her nails into my desk, leaving marks that would stay there forever. I don't know why it turned me on so much, but by God, it turned me on.

"Ninety!" Blossom squeezed out. Then followed several quick blows that brought her to the brink of madness. "Ninety-five!"

Then I paused and tortured her with the uncertainty of the last five strokes. Every little breath of air that hit her sensitive skin made her groan.

"Ninety-six!" she shouted as I swung wide. "Ninety-seven!"

Three more strokes, then I had to get back to work and somehow clear my head of her, because otherwise I'd leave her bent over my desk all day.

"Ninety-eight!" Her whole body trembled with excitement and I had to scrape together the last bit of self-control not to fuck her immediately.

"Ninety-nine!" One more stroke. We both reached our limit.

"One hundred!" The next second she dropped exhausted on my table and I gave her a moment to collect herself.

"Good girl," I said softly as I stroked her soft, sensitive skin. My jaws ground tightly together as my cock pressed painfully against the fabric of my pants.

I pushed her skirt back into place, then walked to the window and stared outside, not even glancing at the skyline stretching out before me. "Go get us sandwiches. Pastrami, with tomatoes."

I knew Blossom was staring at the bag of sandwiches, but she left my office without talking back.

Good girl.

Chapter Thirteen: How Should I Punish You, Little Dove?

Blossom

Ruby leaned over the bar with a curious look on her face when I went to get a Coke during my break.

"Aren't you going to tell us why you're glowing like that?"

"I'm not beaming," I replied with a shrug.

"Yes, you are; you're glowing at uranium-235 levels." She crossed her arms in front of her chest, then turned to Vince. "Why don't you say something about that?"

"I'm not poking around in a snake's nest with a branch," he said with a growl.

I frowned, while Ruby gasped indignantly. "You can't compare Blossom's love life to a snake pit!"

She put her hands on her hips and threw her long hair, which was tied in a tight ponytail as usual, over her shoulder so that the ends almost brushed against Vince's cheek.

"Not Blossom's love life, but your conversations about it," he explained.

"Then why are we telling you anything at all?" she asked in a provocative tone.

He threw his hands in the air. "I wonder the same thing!"

The longer the two of them argued amicably, the wider my grin grew. But when my gaze wandered to the entrance, the corners of my mouth immediately dropped.

Nolan had just entered the Royal Red. When our eyes met, he approached me and I swallowed hard.

"Blossom." His voice was throaty and his reproving gaze traveled down my red dress, which he hated for reasons that were unclear to me. But I hadn't found the time, let alone the money, to buy a new dress. Apart from that, he might have had power over me in Caldwell Tower, but not here.

"Nolan," I replied, forcing myself to smile. Then I gestured to my friends. "This is Ruby and Vince."

It took Ruby about a second to make the connection between my good mood and Nolan. Vince also seemed to be more observant than he wanted to admit, because when they shook hands, he became serious.

"Nice to meet you, Vince," said Nolan.

"Vincent," he corrected him, clearly marking the battle lines. Nolan was unimpressed and sat down on one of the bar stools.

"A bourbon for my boss, please." I tapped my knuckles on the counter. "This one's on me. Vince has about the best bourbon in town stashed here."

"No bourbon." Nolan put his hand on mine, then directed his words to Ruby. "Water, please."

"Coming right up." Ruby set to work and Vince went to the other end of the bar to serve other customers, never once taking his eyes off us.

"Sorry, I thought you liked bourbon." I tried not to let on that I had put my foot in my mouth again. Why was he giving me such a hard time? And why the hell did I want to please him anyway? He was smug, arrogant, and disinterested, and I had to start accepting that.

"I never drink for pleasure," he said. His expression remained serious, which was especially irritating because I knew for a fact that Nolan drank a bourbon every morning without exception.

"Okay, well your water is on me then," I tried to joke.

But Nolan threw a wrench in the works by tossing a twenty-dollar bill on the counter.

Great. He was being himself again, and I had no idea how I could ever explain to Ruby what was going on between us. Not because it was contractually forbidden, but because I didn't know how to categorize my ambivalent feelings.

To escape the situation, I slipped off the bar stool and took two steps back.

"Then if you'll excuse me, I'll continue playing." Without waiting for an answer, I sat back down at the piano and began to play.

Normally, I didn't need the sheet music for my self-composed songs, preferring to let my eyes wander over the audience enjoying my music. But today I stared stubbornly straight ahead to avoid Nolan's gaze. There was no question that he wasn't thrilled about being left standing there, but what else was I supposed to do?

My body was under his power, which is why I could hardly concentrate on playing. And today of all days, my right hand began to cramp up so much that I had to stop before the last song.

Frustrated, I rubbed my wrist and disappeared from the stage before the applause had died down completely. On my way back to the bar, Nolan intercepted me with a hug, kissing me so hard that I felt dizzy.

Before I realized what was happening, he pushed me down a corridor that led to the laundry and storage rooms.

He grabbed me and pushed me against the wall. He grabbed my neck with his left hand. He didn't squeeze hard enough to take my breath away, but with enough force that I could feel his anger. I hid my right hand behind my back so he wouldn't notice how tense it still was.

"You're really trying to make me lose control, aren't you?" he breathed, close to my ear.

"I really don't know what you mean," I whispered back. He was angry, but the situation still made my skin prickle.

"Are you really trying to tell me that you have no idea what effect you have on the men in this room, in this dress?" His gaze slid down me, along with his hand, which ran across the low neckline on my thigh.

"It's just a dress," I tried to reassure him, but his eyes darkened.

"It's not just a dress, damn it!" He slammed the flat of his palm against the wall. "I want to kill every single guy in that room, because everyone looks at you in a way I don't like."

I didn't understand his jealousy. In my eyes, people came here for Vince's good wine and my decent-enough music. No one was interested in me, or my fate. And certainly not for my body.

At least, that's what I had always thought. But Nolan's statements coincided with Ruby's, which I had always thought were teasing.

"I'm all yours," I said in a serious voice.

"I know." The grip around my neck tightened and my center began to throb. "But the rest of the male world doesn't know."

My whole body shook; a small, depraved part of me loved how rough he was with me.

"We know, nothing else matters," I breathed against his lips.

Nolan's gaze darkened, then a grin played around his lips. "Wrong, it's important. And I'm going to make sure that every single guy here will know that you're mine." His voice was like a rumble of thunder; the air around us grew hotter and hotter.

"Your kiss was statement enough. Everyone saw that I'm yours," I replied. At the last moment, I managed to suppress a sigh that would otherwise have slipped from my lips.

"And everyone's about to hear that you're mine." That wasn't an answer, but a promise that made me dizzy. He couldn't be serious.

"What are you going to do?" I asked breathlessly. My heart jumped wildly against my ribs.

He pushed himself away from the wall and opened the door to the storage room. That was enough of an explanation, but one that I didn't like at all.

"Nolan! We can't—" I began.

"We can and we will," he replied in an iron voice. Why did I find it so sexy when he interrupted me like that?

How did he do that? He turned my morals, my entire world view upside down, and I liked it.

"Vince is going to fire me," I continued, desperately trying to come up with excuses for myself as to why this was wrong. Wronger than wrong. Forbidden.

"He won't." Nolan shook his head.

"What if he does?" I asked. Nolan was right, Vince would never fire me for something like that. At least not the first time. There was a better chance of him pulling out the secret shotgun he had hidden under the bar and storming into the storeroom.

"If he kicks you out, I'll buy his bar so you can keep playing." He looked at me, deadly serious. "In a different outfit."

"Do men really stare at me?" I asked, stunned, because I just couldn't understand that it was true. He took my hand and placed it on the hardest part of his body, causing heat to shoot up my cheeks.

"Does that answer your question?" He clenched his jaw, making no secret of the fact that he was angry.

"Yes," I gasped.

Oh my God. When did I finally realize that Nolan was really serious when he said something?

With one swift movement, he pulled the dress off my shoulders. I reflexively hid my arms behind my back until he looked at me, shaking his head.

"You're perfect, little dove. Stop hiding from me."

There was so much sincerity in his words that it almost brought tears to my eyes. He was the first person not to look at me with pity, even though he knew the gritty details of my old life, and for that I was eternally grateful.

Even though there was a chance that he wasn't interested. The relationship between us was based on a contract, I could never forget that. It was dangerous to give in to the illusion that he felt more for me than sexual attraction.

He picked me up by the legs and pressed me against the wall to kiss me.

"How do you want me to punish you, little dove?" Nolan pushed me harder against the wall so that he had one hand free to run over my cheek.

"I don't know," I answered honestly, because I had no experience. Neither with dominant men, nor with what I really liked. "You decide."

He grinned at me. "Next time you should choose your own punishment, because I will always be merciless, and always push you to your limits, because I love your sweet cries."

His fingers traveled along my neck, down to my collarbone. My heart beat even faster against my ribs. It was new to me that someone could trigger such strong feelings in me.

"Will it get less intense at some point?" I asked, more to myself than to Nolan, who was frowning at me.

"What?" He raised a brow questioningly without pausing his exploration of my body with his fingers.

"This tingling all the way to my fingertips," I tried to explain.

He smiled. "It gets more intense every time."

"And if not?" I asked curiously. His face immediately darkened and I regretted my question.

"If this feeling fades or disappears completely, then it's time to dissolve the contract. The same applies if your feelings become too strong," he said coolly.

I shuddered. My feelings were already stronger than they should be...

"Too strong?" I furrowed my brow. I didn't want to ask, because I was afraid of the answer, but I couldn't help it.

"When you fall in love." He looked deep into my eyes, as if he was looking for signs that I had long since fallen in love with him. I avoided his gaze.

"What if you fall in love with me?" I asked after a long silence.

"Don't be ridiculous." His reply was like a punch in the gut, causing my heart to contract painfully.

"Am I not lovable?" I asked quietly.

"No, little dove." He clutched my chin and forced me to look at him again. "I'm not capable of love, that's all."

Something in his face told me that he was perfectly capable of falling in love, he just wouldn't let himself.

But it didn't matter. I wasn't going to fall in love with Nolan anyway and I vowed to end it before I got my heart broken. It had taken forever to pull myself out of the last hole, I certainly wasn't going to be pushed into another one.

He rubbed his hardness, which was pressing against the fabric of his trousers, against my center, and I inhaled sharply. My sensitive pearl pulsed harder and harder and I leaned my head back and closed my eyes.

I started to unbutton his shirt, but he pushed my hands aside. Touching was forbidden unless he allowed me to. It was in his stupid contract. I hadn't thought about it at first, but now I regretted not negotiating more stubbornly, because I really wanted to touch him. Not just touch him, I wanted to get under his skin.

To my surprise, he loosened his tie and put it around my neck. Then he guided my wrists up as well and tied them together so that he could make sure I didn't break any of his rules. The harder I pulled, the more it cut off my air. I hated him for it, but at the same time I couldn't deny that everything was tingling and I was on the verge of losing my mind.

In the meantime, Nolan opened his pants and rubbed himself against my entrance.

"Look at me while I fuck you," he whispered and I obeyed.

I looked deep into his eyes as he penetrated me. Hard. Deep. Full of anger and desire because I had broken his rules. Was I a bad girl because I secretly liked it when he looked at me so darkly? And was I a bad girl because I was thinking about how I could drive him up the wall next?

I was definitely a bad, bad girl and maybe I was enjoying it a tad too much, but it was too late to undo it. I had tasted blood and now I wanted more of it. All of it. Whatever else Nolan did to me, I knew I was going to hate it and love it at the same time.

The harder he took me, the harder I found it to stay calm, and the more his dark brown irises were swallowed up by the black of his pupils.

"I said you were going to scream for me," he gasped, between thrusts. "And I'm not going to stop before then."

I bit my lips, but it wasn't long before I started to moan. He was just too big and too deep inside me to take it in silence. With every thrust, I was less able to hold back until he made his prophecy come true.

I screamed so loudly that the whole club had to hear that I was his. It shouldn't turn me on, but it did. And how. I was on the verge of an orgasm and my heart was fluttering with pleasure. Not just because Nolan was giving me the most intense orgasms of my life, but because he had probably forgotten to punish me beforehand.

But just before I came, he stopped and the waves that had heralded an orgasm ebbed away. Only when I had relaxed did he continue, pushing me to the limits of my mind again until my legs cramped up. Half a second before I came again, he stopped and I realized that this was my punishment.

Again and again he brought me to ecstasy before he dropped me. Until he came himself and buttoned his pants again. I could barely stand, which is why I continued to cling to his shoulders.

"What about me?" I asked, whimpering.

"You ignored my request to change your dress twice. And now I'll make sure it doesn't happen a third time," he replied seriously. "You will not touch yourself until I allow you to. And I probably won't until you get yourself a new dress."

I took a breath to protest, but he put his finger on my lips.

"Trust me, I'll know when you're lying to me in the morning. So don't push it and just accept that your orgasms are mine, and you'll only get them if you're a good girl."

Chapter Fourteen: That Was Not a Compliment

Nolan

As we left the meeting room, I exhaled with relief. The air in there had started to get stuffy, and it wasn't just the board's calcified views that were making me boil.

It was all the unnecessary discussions because they basically had nothing to say against my or Dylan's arguments.

"Did you cancel the four o'clock appointment?" I asked.

Blossom nodded eagerly. "Yes, sir, immediately, as soon as it became clear that it would take longer," she replied.

"Thank you." I called the elevator, pressing the button impatiently. To make matters worse, one of our lawyers that we had been counting on had backed out, and now we had to find another. Even though the biggest merger in East Coast history was going smoothly, and the lawyer thing was just a drop in the bucket, it made my blood boil.

I hated it when things didn't go according to plan. And I hated it even more when I had to assign tasks to people I didn't know.

"Cancel the appointment afterward too," I said as we got into the elevator.

Blossom looked at me, frowning. "We'll definitely be at Caldwell Tower on time."

"No, we won't." I pressed my documents into her hand and stared straight ahead, trying not to get any ideas.

When I was in a mood like this, I found it hard to keep my composure. I usually went to the Haven for that, but I had something even more important on my mind.

Once we arrived on the first floor, Blossom canceled the next appointment, then blinked at me in confusion as I waited for her.

"You could have left long ago," she said with a shrug. She could weave through traffic faster on her motorcycle than I could in my Porsche, which I was driving temporarily because my car was still being painted. In Europe. Because there was no longer a body shop in the U.S. that did this special paint, and business was so good that I hadn't been able to convince the guys to fly to the East Coast with the necessary stuff.

"We have another appointment," I replied, emphasizing the "we". Her eyes widened.

"Oh yeah?" She gave me a questioning look, but I didn't answer her.

I usually parked my car right outside the company, and nobody had a problem with that. But today I had driven into the underground garage, where we would be protected from prying eyes that would have disturbed Blossom.

We stopped in front of my Porsche.

"Get in," I growled. She faltered, but before she could protest, I cut her off with a wave of my hand. "Get in the car, Blossom. We're not leaving until you're ready."

I opened the passenger door, and then walked around the car and got behind the wheel. It took forever for her to sit down with me and close the door, breathing heavily.

"Why?" she asked, obviously in agony. "Is this your sadism coming out again?"

I didn't know how much humor was in her statement, but judging by her trembling tone, it was the pure, cynical truth in her eyes.

"No." I leaned back and stared straight ahead.

"Then why this fuss?"

"Buckle up." After putting my hands on the steering wheel, I waited for her to take her seatbelt and fasten it. But she didn't make it any further than across her chest before she threw it off with a curse.

"Streptopelia turtur. Columba livia. Streptopelia decaocto," she murmured softly. Then her lips continued to move silently.

"Do I need to say more?" I asked, looking at her meaningfully. "We're putting on this show, as you call it, because I want you to be able to drive again yourself."

"Why?" She looked at me with a mixture of bewilderment and surprise.

I swallowed. "Because it's important for your fucking job."

To be honest, I didn't know why I was helping her. There were therapists who would do a better job for sure. Or not, if I took a closer look at Blossom's behavior. In any case, it wasn't the whole truth that it was all about the job, but where the other truths lay, I couldn't say either.

"Sure, of course," she mumbled, making herself even smaller in the seat. "How long are we staying here?" She looked around the car as if it were a death trap that was about to snap shut at any moment.

"I've already told you that," I replied.

"I doubt I'll be cured in half an hour," she pointed out, and I forgave her the sarcasm she was throwing around. I had backed her into a corner, and now she had nothing else to defend herself with.

"Me too. But you underestimate my stubbornness," I replied. Someone had to do something about her fear. She couldn't spend her whole life avoiding every car.

"I was afraid of that." She sighed heavily.

With every minute we spent in the car, it didn't get better, it got worse. Her breathing was irregular and rapid, while her hands clutched her clothes so tightly that the small holes began to appear.

When I finally moved my hand toward the ignition, she flinched. But I had no intention of driving off. She was nowhere near ready.

"I'm not going to drive anywhere until you're strapped in," I said dryly. Then I switched on some music.

When she recognized her own song, she blinked at me in surprise.

"Spotify," I explained as her questioning gaze continued to pierce me.

"Oh. I should have known that," she replied. Her music seemed to calm her down. In any case, her breathing became a little shallower, and her fingers only rubbed at the fabric of her clothes instead of piercing it with her nails.

"Do you want to talk about something?" I offered. "Sometimes it helps to talk about things to take your mind off something else."

Blossom shrugged. She was clearly one of those women who silently absorbed everything, instead of exploding or babbling when she was nervous.

"Birds, for example. How did you become interested?" I was even more curious as to why she habitually listed the Latin names of all the urban pigeons that existed in New York.

"Believe me, I definitely don't want to talk about pigeons right now. I'm just thinking about them." She laughed hysterically.

I had no idea what she was talking about, but people in panic mode never acted rationally, I could say that from personal experience. I had a loose theory about what the pigeons were all about, but as long as my little dove didn't talk about it, I was still in the dark.

"Do you want to talk about music?" I continued, keeping my voice steady.

She turned to me. "Why are you staying so calm?" she asked. Her gaze slid down to meet mine. "Sure, you never yell, but your everyday tone runs the gamut from 'the world is gray and bleak' to 'I want to watch the world burn'. But you're actually unflappable, even though I'm a terrible assistant and you're missing two meetings because of me." Tears watered up in her emerald eyes.

"I want to help you."

She shook her head. "Don't say it's self-serving, so that I can work better with you. We both know that's a lie, or at least not entirely true. So why are you doing this for me? Why do you feel obligated, when you could obviously care less?" She tilted her head, causing her high braid to fall over her shoulder.

"I do care," I replied sternly. The world thought I was an unapproachable asshole, and I probably was. But that didn't mean I didn't give a shit.

"Why?" she asked.

I knew that this whole thing was confusing for her. For me too. I wasn't acting like myself. But if there was one thing I'd learned from

Donnie, it was that if you see a problem somewhere, and you have a solution to it, you help.

"Because I care about you, little dove." I put a hand on her thigh to show how serious I was. My answer made her inhale sharply.

"What is this between us?" She tried to find an answer on my face, but failed. No one could get through my facade easily.

"I don't know. But now is not a good time to discuss it," I blocked out. This was her therapy, not mine.

"I thought I was supposed to talk to distract myself?" she asked, giving me a challenging look.

"About other things," I countered.

"Because you don't talk about feelings?"

I nodded, and her brows drew together as if she'd had a flash of insight.

"Then we should use this car therapy thing to treat us both. I'll treat the fear of driving, and you use the chance to talk about your feelings." She smiled at me, and when a new song started on the playlist, she closed her eyes briefly and took a deep breath. "This was the first song I finished writing without ever reworking it. In fact, it's the only song I've never revised. I wrote it on the first day of college."

There seemed to be a happy memory attached to it.

"Didn't you have to learn how to write music at college first?" I asked. I didn't know much about the world of professional music, which for me was only divided into two categories. I either liked it or I didn't like it. There was nothing in between.

"I've been writing songs all my life. But this one is something special." Her foot tapped to the beat of the music; her eyes remained closed. "I haven't heard it for a long time."

"Why didn't you rework it like the others?" I asked. It seemed to calm her down to talk about the music.

"Because it's perfect. Because I knew then that going to university was the right thing to do, and that it would be my future." She sighed heavily, and the sadness in her eyes made me swallow hard. We both knew that her dream of this future had died. Irrevocably and cruelly.

Blossom turned off the music and bit the insides of her cheeks, hard enough for me to see. I gave her a moment to collect herself.

"Now we're talking about you. Or rather, about your feelings," she said, returning to the point of the conversation that made my whole body tense up.

"No." I put my hands around the steering wheel and the longer she stared at me, the tighter my grip became.

"Why?" she asked, confused. It was quite normal for her to talk about her feelings all day long. But she should also know better than anyone that there were things you didn't want to talk about.

"Because I have no feelings," I replied coolly.

"Now you're making a fool of yourself," she said, using my own line against me.

"I'm still your boss. You shouldn't forget that," I growled. Besides, there was another contract between us and if she carried on like this, I would be forced to use those rules against her too.

"You can't deny that you feel something. Otherwise you wouldn't be doing this."

Shit. I couldn't get anything out of such indirect orders, on the contrary, they made me angry.

"I'm not going to talk to you about my feelings. Period." I stared at her sternly until she avoided my gaze and rolled her eyes.

"This was a really stupid idea." She opened the car door and was about to get out, but I grabbed her wrist.

"I don't talk about my problems. I deal with my issues differently," I explained. I couldn't bring myself to say any more, but it seemed to be enough for her to stay.

"So you have problems too?" It was more of a statement than a question, but she still seemed surprised. Admittedly, I was good at hiding anything that could have been seen as a weakness.

"Everyone has to carry their own baggage. Some people show it more, others less," I replied.

"You don't look like someone with baggage," Blossom replied thoughtfully. Her eyes flew over my body again, as if the answer was there somewhere.

"Thank you." I nodded at her.

"That wasn't a compliment. Rather the opposite," she mumbled.

"Why is it bad if no one sees your weaknesses?" I asked. I didn't expect an answer to the question because it was meant rhetorically, but she seemed to feel obliged to answer.

"Because then there's no one there to see you break, so you can't be saved." She spoke her words with such conviction, and I wondered how much she was relating these words to herself. There were obviously things she needed to be saved from, but no one had helped her.

"I don't need to be rescued. Don't worry about me, little dove." I stroked a strand of hair out of her face.

I hadn't expected this conversation to go in such a direction. I found my balance in the Haven, but neither the conversations with Bruce and Dylan, nor the fights, had triggered anything like Blossom's words. Or her looks.

Fuck. I had imagined it differently and we definitely needed different rules for the next time. No feelings. No fucking feelings.

"You can get out," I heard myself say as the words left my mouth.

"Already?" She sounded almost sad.

"That's enough for now. Besides, we still have five hours of work ahead of us." I kept quiet about the fact that it was me, not her, who was having a hard time sitting here in the damn car with her and pretending everything was fine.

"Whatever happened," I began, leaving a short pause. "You can get over it."

"Of course, sir." She got out, looking relieved, but there was also something I interpreted as sadness in her face, which turned into wounded pride before she slammed the door and I could finally breathe again.

Chapter Fifteen: Don't Be Angry Because I Am the Way I Am

Blossom

I fanned myself with a stack of papers I pulled out of the photocopier. The afternoon air was hot and oppressive, and the outfits I had to wear to keep Nolan reasonably happy weren't exactly breathable.

There was air conditioning in Caldwell Tower, and a fan on my desk blew air at me, groaning bravely all the while, but the air in the copy room was thick enough to cut, and if Nolan kept this up, I'd spend my workday in the copy room on the sixteenth floor because the copier on the executive floor kept eating the paper.

On the way back to his office, I wiped the sweat from my forehead with the back of my hand. It wasn't just the heat that bothered me, but also the fact that clouds were slowly but surely building up over the city, heralding a storm. I hated thunderstorms.

Streptopelia turtur. Columba livia. Streptopelia decaocto.

Just the thought of rain made my heart beat painfully against my ribs. There was nothing worse than rain.

My gaze drifted over to Nolan. As usual, he was hunched over his laptop and paying no attention to me. Which wasn't as bad as the looming rain, but it was almost as bad.

He was alone, and he had been ignoring me since I got out of his car. I had no idea if it was because I couldn't tell him everything, or because there were things he didn't talk about either, but something had happened. Something that I couldn't quite put into words, and that confused him as much as it confused me.

Something was different between us. Somehow our working relationship had gotten out of hand, because there were feelings that I couldn't describe. When he was fucking my brains out, he was different than he was now. And since I'd spent time with him in his rental car, there was a third, even more unapproachable version of him.

"The documents," I said, putting the papers down.

"Thank you." That was all he said. Taciturn as always. By the time I'd gotten the panic attack in his car halfway under control, he had made me realize that I wasn't the only one with problems. Now I couldn't stop wondering what was bothering him, and why he never talked about it. That had become clear when he had literally thrown me out of the car after dropping his facade for a second.

"You're staring," he said.

"Oh, sorry." I winced, fiddling with the hem of my long sleeve. I was about to walk out of the office when Nolan propped his elbows on the desk and looked at me.

"You've been staring at me this whole time. Why?"

"Not important." I shrugged and tried to look unconcerned. My pulse raced because he had noticed my gaze. Not just noticed, he was bothered by it.

"You're a bad liar."

Actually, I was a pretty good liar when it came to things like that.

I'm fine. Everything is excellent. I'm happy.

Lies that everyone said all the time and were believed, no matter how obviously false they were. Lies that were so polished that they shouldn't hurt when you spoke them, but the splinters still stung painfully, and cut deep into the heart.

"If you keep looking at me like that, I'll be forced to fire you. And I really don't need to be looking for a new assistant right now," he growled. "So spit out what's been on the tip of your tongue the whole time."

"Why are you like this?" I bit my lower lip, trying not to think about getting kicked out of his car, which had hurt me more than I wanted to admit.

"Everyone has to be something, it's called character," he replied coolly.

I snorted softly. "You know exactly what I mean. Why is it that sometimes you're so charming that you make me feel like you care about me, and then suddenly you're ice cold and so unpredictable that I think you're your own evil twin?"

He looked at me but didn't answer, so I continued.

"You order me to sit in your car to cure my anxiety, and you do that because you have a heart. Because you want me to feel better. Don't you? I can't possibly be imagining that."

He was silent again, but this time the silence was a good thing, because it also meant that he wasn't protesting.

"What do you want to hear from me now?" He stood up and walked around the desk toward me. "Do you want to hear that I'm madly in love with you? Do you want me to promise you the moon, and let you believe that we'll be together forever? If that's what you want, I'm going to have to disappoint you. I'm not capable of that. Feelings are not my strong point and they never will be."

Every single word was spat in contempt, and they cut into my heart. I was too grown up, too rational to believe in Prince Charming anymore, but that didn't mean I had given up hope of finding someone to spend my life with.

I narrowed my eyes. "I don't want any false promises and I don't want any lies. I just want the truth, that's all," I whispered.

"That's more than most people will ever get," he replied. His eyes turned icy cold and I knew, in that moment, that he hadn't been born this way. The world had made him what he was. That didn't make the situation any better, because if he broke my heart—and he definitely had heart-breaking potential—then it didn't matter what the reason was. Broken was broken. Still, that realization was important to me, because if it was all a facade, there was a chance I could tear it down to see the real Nolan behind it.

"What happened to you to make you like this?" The question just slipped out, there was nothing I could do about it. But now the damage was done.

"We're not going to talk about it because there's nothing to talk about." He glared at me and clenched his hands into fists so tightly that his knuckles stood out white. That was the end of the discussion. But it also made me realize that there was indeed something that needed to be discussed.

He didn't say it, but something from his past was still haunting him. I knew the feeling only too well, because I also ran away from things that haunted me, again and again. And sometimes I had the feeling that we, the rushed ones, recognized each other and were somehow connected. A small comfort, but at least it sometimes gave me the feeling that I wasn't as alone as I felt.

Sometimes it felt like the hardest thing in the world not to think about the past; I felt ridiculous that the only thing that helped me cope with my anxiety was the stupid pigeon counting.

That... and Nolan. I'd spent more time in a car with him than I had in a long time. Not only that, but in the end I'd almost stopped being scared. Of course, I was still an eternity away from driving again, but it was more progress than I'd ever made.

"If you ever think about..." I began, but he raised his hand, his eyes stormy as the sky outside.

"I forbid you to ever ask about my past again. You work for me. You are my personal assistant and my sub. Nothing more. Understood?"

Wow. This message has been clearly received.

"Yes, sir," I replied tonelessly, so that he wouldn't notice how shaken I was.

His features immediately softened again. "Be a good girl and don't poke around in wasp's nests. You'll only get stung."

I nodded, still unable to say anything. I avoided his gaze by letting my eyes wander over the skyline, which was perfectly visible from his office window.

He stood in front of me and lifted my chin with his thumb and forefinger.

"Don't be angry because I am the way I am, little dove."

I wanted to stay mad at him, but how could I resist him when he looked at me like that? Maybe it was stupid. No, not just maybe, it was definitely stupid, but I kept going back to him, even though I knew it would end in a broken heart.

I nodded, then cleared my throat to get rid of the frog stuck inside.

"I should get everything ready for the appointment with Mr. Mercer now." I pointed clearly toward the door; I wanted to leave here as quickly as possible.

"Dylan never comes on time, we still have time," Nolan rebuked me.

"Time for what?" I furrowed my brow.

"Time for me to show you where your place is." He pushed me to the edge of his desk, then pushed my shoulders down so that I had to get on my knees. Smiling contentedly, he sat down in his chair and scooted close to me so that I was trapped between him and the desk.

I didn't blame him for wanting to avoid the conversation. We all had our ways and means. I mean pigeons and he had petty sex. But who was I kidding? Sex was no longer trivial for me, in fact it had never been trivial.

As I went downstairs and tried to make myself half comfortable under the table, I heard my heart breaking in the distance.

"Look at me," he whispered. When our eyes met, I forgot what I had just been thinking about. His dark eyes scrutinized me, there was a lopsided smile on his lips and the dominance that oozed from his every pore made my skin tingle.

He was really good at taking my mind off things.

Nolan opened his pants and I inhaled sharply as his hardness jumped out at me. I unconsciously bit my lips, which he commented on with a growl, before he grabbed my hair and pulled me against him.

"You know what I want." I opened my mouth and concentrated fully on how his firm grip was guiding me.

"Touch yourself," he continued to murmur and my hand slipped under the black skirt I was wearing. I groaned out. "Good girl."

What we were doing was so forbidden and so good that I kept moaning against his hardness. Nolan watched me the whole time and every time I wanted to turn away from him, he commanded me to return his gaze.

Oh God. Every time I thought he had set the bar at the top, he came along and blew it out of all proportion.

He penetrated me deeper and deeper. So deep that the tip of my nose pressed against his six-pack and I couldn't breathe. A small part of me rebelled at the way Nolan was using me, but most of me idolized him for it because I didn't want to be treated any differently. I wanted him to use me. I don't know what was wrong with me, or if everything was okay, but that's the way it was.

"Fuck, Blossom," he cursed softly as he pressed me all the way against him, forcing me to stay in position until my eyelids fluttered. Not much longer and I came too. My pearl was so sensitive that the breeze was almost enough to make me come.

A tear ran down my cheek that I didn't know where it had come from, but it didn't seem to bother him. He wiped it away with his thumb, smiled and then let me slide back far enough to breathe again.

Then he sank himself completely into me again and looked at me seriously. "I want to see you come, little dove."

I nodded, I couldn't answer any other way. When he loosened his grip again and I gasped gratefully, two things happened.

The door was pulled open first, which made me flinch. But Nolan's reaction to this irritated me even more. Instead of letting go of me and pushing me under the table, his grip tightened again and he pushed me against him again. Oh. My. God.

I was hidden under the table, which was closed at the front, but you could still see me from certain angles, and hear me from all directions.

What was he thinking? He didn't look like he was worried, on the contrary, he seemed to be enjoying the heat shooting up my cheeks.

"You're on time," he said tonelessly.

"And you're making the most obvious points again," Dylan replied just as dryly. "Where's the girl?"

"Busy." He looked down at me. "She has something for me to do. And she knows what happens if I'm not perfectly happy."

I knew immediately what he meant, but he couldn't be serious! Now? Here, with his hardness in my mouth and his business partner on the other side of the table.

I got so dizzy that I no longer knew which way was up and which way was down.

Yes, he meant it. At the latest when his grip hardened and he sank deeper into me again, I realized that he expected me to obey his command.

Dylan sighed. "You shouldn't always shoo them like that."

"She likes it," he replied and I was about to protest.

"Whatever you say." Dylan sounded as unconvinced as I was. He sat down on one of the leather chairs in front of the table and I relaxed a little.

I had no idea how he managed to keep talking about the business during the blowjob, but he did. He kept throwing out figure after figure. Statistics here, quarterly forecasts there.

"My assistant should hurry up," growled Nolan. To emphasize his impatience, he drummed his fingertips on the tabletop.

"You could ask Karen, she's loitering outside the door."

"That's all right," Nolan waved her off. "She knows that I attach great importance to punctuality."

My whole body was vibrating and I was about to climax. My anger at him only fueled the tingling of my center. I hated him for not usually letting me come so easily and now I hated him for insisting on an orgasm.

But what I hated most was that he had this effect on me, where just one look took my breath away and just hearing his name gave me goosebumps.

Nolan pressed me firmly against him and I struggled not to make a telltale noise. The tension grew and when he smiled at me secretly from above, I lost my self-control.

I gave in to the crazy sensations, massaging my pearl and imagining that it was his hand touching me while he took my mouth.

He moved my head back and forth, sinking deeper and deeper into me until he came and I had no choice but to take in every drop. And that did the rest. His hardness in my mouth stifled my moans as I came and he patted my cheek contentedly.

I zipped up his pants and crawled deeper under the table until they both decided to continue their conversation over a sandwich at Daisy's.

It wasn't until I was quite sure that they had both left the building that I crawled out from under the table, smoothed out my clothes and grabbed the papers that Nolan had just put on to copy for Dylan.

When I left the office, I almost ran into Karen, who was standing in the middle of the corridor taking selfies.

"I didn't even see you in the office," she said snidely.

"Well noted," I replied with a grin, because I couldn't help but give her a little side blow. She had long since made it clear that she hated me and I didn't want to waste energy trying to convince her otherwise. People like Karen were just... Karen.

"The tide will turn at some point, you'll see," she called after me.

Nevertheless, I couldn't stop grinning, because the last waves of my climax were still dancing through my system. He hadn't said it out loud, but the look in his eyes said it all. And that was all I wanted to hear from him.

Good girl.

Chapter Sixteen: You Are More Than That

Nolan

Blossom got in the car and handed me a paper bag from Daisy's.

"Extra pastrami, extra tomatoes," she said with a smile. When she looked out through the windshield and saw the clouds hanging over the city, her face became serious again.

"It's time for a thunderstorm," I said, sighing as I bit into my sandwich. The heat was slowly getting to everyone's head.

"I wouldn't mind if the storm stayed away," she mumbled and unwrapped her sandwich. By now, we had spent so much time in the car that she could hold normal conversations without having panic attacks. And we had both slowly come to terms with the fact that we spent our daily lunch break in the car.

Now that the merger with Dylan and Bruce was almost complete, I could perhaps carve out some more time, because Blossom was slowly making progress.

"Isn't the heat driving you crazy?" I asked in surprise.

"Yes, it is. But I don't particularly like thunderstorms." With a shrug, she put her sandwich on the dashboard and pulled one knee up to her chest to rest her chin on it. I looked at her with a raised eyebrow.

"What?" she asked indignantly. "I took my shoe off." She wiggled her toes demonstratively.

"I didn't say anything," I replied and carried on eating.

"But you were thinking so loudly that half of New York could hear." She pierced me with a reproachful look that left me cold.

"You're imagining things." I didn't say any more, because I didn't have anything else to say.

"In that case." She slipped her other shoe and pulled her second leg onto the leather seat. Her skirt slid dangerously far up. So far that I could see that she was adhering to the no-slip rule.

"If you don't want me to fuck you on the spot, you should choose a different position that is less provocative," I said in a sharp tone of voice.

Her legs immediately shot back into the footwell and she adjusted her skirt.

"Don't you want to be fucked by me?" I asked in a throaty voice. My question made her cheeks flush as she stammered confusedly, trying to get out of the question somehow.

"It's okay, little dove. I was just teasing you." I grinned at her and she began to giggle.

"Since when do you make jokes?" She looked me up and down. Her posture was relaxed, so I leaned back and continued to stare at the towering clouds that were slowly moving over the city, heralding a huge thunderstorm.

Hopefully it wouldn't be too much longer before the cooling rain finally arrived to provide relief from the heat. The longer I sat here with Blossom, the more I felt like I couldn't think straight.

"Good question," I replied thoughtfully. Now that she pointed it out to me, I hardly recognized myself. I hadn't been this relaxed for ages. Not even after the Haven.

"I used to make jokes all the time," I said spontaneously before I could moderate myself. I was like a different person around her. A person who was less broken.

"You? I can't imagine that at all." She looked at me as if I were a complete stranger.

"It's been ages. And a lot has changed," I explained soberly.

"Times change," she replied in a tone that made me shudder.

"And people too," I added to her statement.

Shit. I had definitely changed. Nevertheless, I never asked myself what would have become of me if my parents hadn't fucked it up so badly.

"Wow. This has been a pretty deep lunch," she murmured. She fiddled thoughtfully with the hem of her skirt, as she always did when she didn't know where to put her hands.

"You fidget too much, you know that, right?" I asked. She immediately placed her hands on her thighs with her palms facing up. She smiled proudly when I nodded.

"Fasten your seatbelt," I said, trying to make it sound less like a command than a request.

"Now?" she gasped.

I still thought it was a good idea. She was strong enough, and she had gained enough confidence to risk it.

"Try it, I know you can do it," I continued.

With a sweeping gesture to stall for time, she grabbed the belt and pulled it forward.

"Good girl."

Everything looked fine, but just before the click, she faltered and closed her eyes to better control her breathing.

"What a bummer," she whispered, cursing, not moving another inch.

I put my hand on hers. It was a gesture I had to force myself to make, because physical closeness wasn't my strong point. But her grateful look was worth it.

She still couldn't put the seatbelt in the lock, but she didn't run from the car, which could definitely be seen as further progress.

"Tell me something." I nodded at her.

"What am I supposed to say?" Her eyes wandered around the car as if there was an answer somewhere.

"Something about you," I suggested. We worked together every day, but she never talked about anything. Except when she was excited. Then it just gushed out of her, but it was usually so incoherent and chaotic that I couldn't understand any of it.

"There's not much to say about me." She chewed on her lower lip and looked at the skyscrapers in front of us.

"You're wrong," I contradicted her, my tone so serious that she looked at me in surprise.

"Oh yeah?" Frowning, she waited for an explanation. I could tell she didn't believe me, and didn't expect me to have anything else to say, but she was wrong. I had a hell of a lot to say, I just couldn't.

"Yes," I replied with a nod.

She gave me a sheepish smile. "Thank you, it's a kind gesture, but I know I'm nothing special."

She swiped her free hand through her hair, avoiding my gaze. But I wasn't going to be brushed off that easily. Especially not from my sub. I growled softly and she immediately looked me in the eye again.

"You have an unmistakable smile that can't be found anywhere else in the world. Your smile is as unmistakable as your eyes," I replied.

Blossom put her hand to her face. "What color eyes do I have?"

"Green," I answered without missing a beat. I knew her eyes, not only because I stared at them for hours every day, but because they haunted me when I slept.

"Okay, lucky guess," she mumbled, blushing.

"When the sun is shining, the brown rim around your pupils is even more visible than it already is. And when you're sad but try to hide it, the bright green of your eyes also disappears, and they suddenly look gray and colorless. But I find them most beautiful when you play the piano, because then they shine like emeralds. When you play and..." I faltered when I heard my own words.

She swallowed hard, clearly my answer had surprised her. In fact, we were both surprised at my sincerity.

"You know my eyes really well," she said in a strained voice.

"You should know by now that I mean everything I say." I put my sandwich to one side and wiped my hands on a napkin.

"In some respects, I believe you right away."

"In all cases." That wasn't just a phrase, I meant it. I meant everything I said. Everything without exception. If there was one thing I had learned, it was that wishful thinking was useless. Clear statements, on the other hand, led to a goal, or at least you didn't tread water.

I took a deep breath. Something had been on my mind for a while that I wanted to tell her. "Blossom, listen to me. The other day, in the office, when I yelled at you..."

"You need to be a bit more specific. With all due respect, you're a really lousy boss," she interrupted me dryly.

"When I forbid you to talk about my past," I continued, and she immediately became serious again. "I shouldn't have shouted at you."

"It's okay, you didn't want to talk about it, and I didn't stop probing. It's none of my business." She shrugged. "I'm just your employee."

"You're more than that." My muscles hardened as I realized that she had this attitude because I showed her nothing else.

"Okay, I'm still your sub too," she replied with a shrug. She seemed to have accepted the fact that she didn't think she was good enough for me, and my body stiffened even more. Had I really become that kind of person?

I squeezed her hand tighter.

"Nolan?" she asked, gazing at me again with that innocent look that made me want to rip her clothes off immediately.

"Blossom?" I looked at her expectantly.

She blinked rapidly. "Why did you want me to sign your contract?

I had asked myself the same question a thousand times.

"I wanted to make sure you could pay your debts."

She tilted her head and looked at me, disappointed. "You know I'm talking about the *other* contract. The one you were standing in my apartment with in the middle of the night."

Of course I knew what she was talking about, but I still didn't know why exactly I'd been at her door, or why I'd insisted she text me every night when she got home. Hell, I didn't know why we sat here every damn day, hoping her anxiety would slowly fade.

"I don't know," I confessed honestly.

"That's not an answer." Her look was a direct challenge.

"I can't give you a better one." I had asked myself exactly the same question hundreds of times. In vain.

"Something inside you blows all my fuses. You're not really my type, not as an assistant or as a sub," I tried to explain what was going on inside me.

"How charming. As a woman, you like to hear non-compliments like that," she gritted from behind clenched teeth. "I'll try not to take it personally, just like your behavior in the office. You just can't help yourself."

I looked at her seriously until the cynical expression on her face had disappeared.

"Normally I only sleep with women who have signed a contract. Faceless women without names or features. They come uncomplicated, I fuck them uncomplicated, and they leave uncomplicated, without me remembering them. The thing with you is not uncomplicated. If you hadn't signed that night, I would have fucked you anyway."

I had never shown so much sincerity before, and I resolved not to repeat it; I hated the feeling of showing weakness. And how weak did you have to be to fabricate words like that?

Fucking weak, Caldwell. Disappointingly weak. It wasn't my voice echoing in my head, it was my father's, but that didn't make it any better.

Blossom looked at me meaningfully, and I expected a novel, but she only said a single word.

"Why?" Her pupils widened and she tilted her head, causing her hair to slide down her cheek in such a way that I had the reflex to brush it out of her face again.

I gritted my teeth. "We should change the subject."

"No. Don't do this." She shook her head and looked at me pleadingly, but I had long since finished with the subject.

"Enough for today." I sliced my hand through the air as if I could cut out the thoughts that were running through my head.

"I'll go to my limits if you go to yours," she said with a determined look. Then she clicked the seatbelt into place and looked at me challengingly.

Fuck. I had underestimated her.

"You don't want to know what's going on inside me, little dove." It was a crystal-clear warning, one that she had better take seriously.

"Yes, I do and that's exactly what you owe me now." She put her hands on her hips. I could see her struggling against the pressure of the seatbelt, but her anger was stronger than her fear.

My hands tensed up and I gripped the steering wheel even tighter.

"Alright, fine by me. One question." That was all I allowed her.

"Do I mean anything to you?" She looked at me hopefully and I hated to dash her hopes.

"I can't love, I've already told you that. Different question."

All of a sudden, I got a hell of a hankering to have a throwdown, no-holes-barred match at Left Hook Haven. Everyone versus me. Hard, but not impossible. And if I did lose, at least they'd beat these feelings out of me that weren't good for me or Blossom.

"Okay, I'll rephrase. Are there any feelings, of any kind, that you have for me?"

"Yes."

She flinched at my answer and looked at me in shock. But I also recognized relief, because she was right with her assumption.

"Then why don't you ever show them to me?" For half a second she wrapped her skirt hem around her finger, but then she corrected herself and turned her palms up again.

"One question. That was the deal. And you got the answer to your question," I replied, more calmly than I felt.

When she realized I was serious, she immediately unfastened her seatbelt and took a deep breath. She suppressed a disappointed sigh because she realized I wasn't going to say anything more and I knew I would regret what I did next. Fuck.

I reached back to pull out a package from Bertani and give it to her.

"For me?" she asked in surprise. I had just made her run into an ice wall, and now I was throwing presents at her.

"I'd look ridiculous in it," I replied as she opened the box to reveal an elegant ball gown.

"What's this for?" She glared at me angrily. "If it's for the Royal Red, you know I'll still be wearing my old dress." Her fingers glided over the rose-colored fabric, which was embroidered with pearls, crystals, and diamonds.

"I know. And you know I'll punish you for every single day you wear it," I replied, which elicited a brief smile from her. "It's for the gala that's coming up to celebrate the successful merger. I want you to come with me."

"As your assistant? Won't I be a bit overdressed?" She held up the dress and examined it critically.

"More than that," I replied.

"As what, exactly?" She dropped the garment back into the box and scrutinized me with narrowed eyes.

I breathed a sigh of relief, because I had given her the answer she had asked for earlier.

"Every single person there will realize that you're mine."

Chapter Seventeen: You're Mine, Little Dove

Blossom

I thought the Caldwell Tower was huge, but it was nothing compared to the estate where Nolan's gala was being held. A huge mansion that stood, in cliche fashion, on top of a mountain, looking down on New York City from above.

I couldn't see a starry sky through the thick, black clouds, but the city below us had a radiant aura due to the night lights, which sent a pleasant shiver down my spine.

After sneaking inside to change out of my riding leathers, I went straight to the balcony next to the checkroom. There I took a deep breath and waited for Nolan.

I knew that he would have preferred to pick me up in a limousine, but it was still too early for that. He hadn't shown his disappointment, but I knew it was there.

We had made progress, but I wasn't ready to ride yet. Especially not on an evening that was as important for him as this one.

When I turned around, he was leaning against the entrance to the balcony, grinning at me. He always looked good as hell, but just now... oh boy. He wore a tailored black suit that emphasized his muscular body as much as his dark eyes. He had a charming smile on his lips that some people, including me, would be willing to sell their souls for.

"You look magical." His gaze wandered down to my body before he sought eye contact again.

"Thank you." I curtseyed a little and pulled up the gloves I was wearing. It had taken me ages to find a pair that matched the color of the dress, but after a half-marathon through New York, Ruby and I had finally found them.

Irritatingly, the dress was almost an exact copy of the red dress that Nolan hated so much. It was very similar, it just had no sleeves.

"Come with me." He held out his hand and I followed him. But instead of going to the event, we walked outside to his limousine, which was parked right in front of the entrance. He opened the back door and gestured for me to get in.

"What's going on?" I asked, confused.

"Get in," he ordered. I opened my mouth to object, but he clicked his tongue in reprove and gave me a stern look that made my core throb.

Reluctantly, but without further objection, I got into the car. He closed the door and then got in on the other side.

I shifted restlessly and waited for an explanation.

"It's part of a gala for a man to help his escort out of the car," he explained to me pointedly. "I'll help you out of the car, then we'll walk down the red carpet together, which leads directly into the main room, and there I'll ask you to dance."

"Sometimes traditions are made to be broken," I mumbled, loud enough for him to hear me.

"I'll remind you of that when I get a chance, little dove." It was a blunt threat that made my whole body tingle, and Nolan knew exactly how I was reacting to it. He just knew me too well; sometimes I wondered where this was all going. On the one hand, he was so cold and distant that it brought tears to my eyes, and then he was all charming again.

I vigorously reminded myself that everything between us only existed because of a contract that he could terminate at any time. Just the thought of the end of our agreement triggered a pang of heartache in my chest that I found hard to shake off. A small part of me feared that he would no longer have any use for me once I had paid off my debt for the scratched car.

"Where are your thoughts?" he asked, lifting my chin with his thumb.

"No big deal." I waved him off, swallowed the last of my uneasy feeling, and forced myself to look him in the eye again.

He took out a small box and gave it to me.

"What's this?" I took the box and shook it gently next to my ear.

"I promised you that everyone would know tonight that you're mine. This is my proof of that." His voice was throaty and he nuzzled my neck as his words made my skin tingle.

I opened the box to reveal a silver chain with a small dove hanging from it.

Wow. That thing had to be worth a fortune. Not only was it unique, but it also had a meaning that only Nolan and I understood. Okay, we had different definitions of pigeons, but thanks to him I now had a different perspective on things. He had changed the way I looked at birds, and the whole world. There was nothing better than being called a little dove by him.

He took the necklace out of the box and put it around my neck. My fingers immediately grasped the dove. I couldn't stop grinning.

"Thank you. This means a lot to me," I whispered, unable to find better words. "Do you know why I recite the names of birds when I'm scared?"

"No." He looked at me curiously, but didn't press me for an answer.

"Shortly after the incident, my psychologist advised me to find a distraction." I took a deep breath. "And there was an encyclopedia about pigeons on his shelf. So I started to memorize it."

It had been ages since I'd been in Rhyan's office, yet I could remember every little detail because I'd spent most of my college years there.

Nolan looked at me, frowning. "What psychologist has an encyclopedia on pigeons on his shelf?"

"I don't know. It didn't seem to matter to Rhyan, otherwise he wouldn't have given me the book," I finally replied with a shrug.

"Rhyan. The name explains everything." Nolan grinned as if I'd made a joke.

"You have to explain that to me," I demanded, confused and hoping for an explanation.

"There's nothing more to say." He nodded to make it clear that he didn't want to add anything else, but I gave him a pout and a pleading look and he sighed in exasperation.

"Any guy named Rhyan is literally crying out to collect pigeon encyclopedias," he explained.

I giggled. "You can't lump all the Rhyans in the world together." I put my hands on my hips, as best my seated position would allow, but he wasn't impressed.

"I can and I have." He got out of the car and opened my door for me. "Now, could I ask the most beautiful woman of the evening to accompany me?" He held out his hand to me, which I accepted, still grinning.

After getting out of the air-conditioned car, the air outside felt oppressive. My gaze briefly wandered to the storm clouds above us, which heralded a huge thunderstorm. That made me feel a little queasy. Then I focused on Nolan again, who led me into the villa like a gentleman.

"I didn't realize how important traditions are to you." I looked at him curiously.

"I want you to remember this evening forever. Because it's special, not because we didn't follow any of the social rules that apply here." The way he emphasized his words made me shudder.

"Why do you attach so much importance to it?" I asked.

He looked so deeply into my eyes that my breath caught in my throat. "You're mine, little dove. It won't always stay that way. But this way I can make sure that part of your memories will continue to belong to me."

My legs went all weak, and I had to concentrate hard not to just fall over because I was so blown away by his words.

"Why should that change?" My heart was beating wildly in my chest. I should say that I felt more for him, but I just didn't dare.

What were the chances of him reciprocating my feelings? What he said sounded suspiciously like feelings, but Nolan was Nolan, and it could also mean that he was just talking about quitting. Who knew what was going on in his head? Sometimes I thought he didn't know himself.

He gave me a half pained smile before answering.

"Because even little doves like you will eventually fly on." His finger stroked my hand, which was resting on his arm, as he led me along the carpet.

"Pigeons are very loyal animals. As long as you don't scare them away, they always come back to their home," I replied. For the first time in my life, all this knowledge about birds had done me some good. But instead of answering, he led me to the entrance of the villa.

I wanted to enter the gala, which was already packed with hundreds of people, but he pulled me a little further and pushed me against the wall.

"I almost forgot one thing," he whispered close to my ear. His fingertips traveled along my cheek, down to my arms. Without further ado, he took off the glove on my left hand and before I knew it, he was pulling the right one down too.

I pulled my arm back and tugged the glove back into place.

"Don't," I whispered.

"How am I supposed to show the men in there that the most beautiful woman of the evening is mine if she's hiding?" He looked at me uncomprehendingly.

"They're just gloves," I replied. I found it hard to concentrate when he was pushing me so hard against the wall. I shouldn't react so strongly to his body, but I did, and there was nothing I could do about it. Instead, I should try to accept that Nolan had a power over me that no man had ever had over me. And I doubted that after him, another man would come into my life who could come close to him in any way.

He shook his head. "It's not just the gloves. We both know that."

I avoided his gaze until he tilted my chin to the side with his thumb, until I was forced to look at him again.

"Stop hiding. You're perfect, Blossom." He breathed a kiss on my lips.

"They're not pretty scars." Instinctively, my finger moved to the spot on my arm where the biggest scar was.

"You're perfect." He said it again, reverently and with conviction. His words made me gasp, because I could tell that he really meant it.

I didn't like it, but I slowly pulled the glove off anyway. More to prove to Nolan that he was wrong, and that my scars bothered him after all, but when I slipped the fabric off my skin, he beamed at me. He had disarmed me and I had no choice but to accept that he was right. Or at least that he believed his own words.

"Good girl," he whispered against my lips. He gathered up my gloves and put them in his pants pocket. He didn't say it out loud, but I knew he'd give them back to me if I couldn't stand it without them. But I at least wanted to try. Nolan believed in me and so far he had always been right in his assumptions. Why should I doubt him now?

He pushed me against the wall one last time, licked my lower lip in a way that almost drove me out of my mind, then he released me and adjusted his suit.

"Ready?" he asked, stretching out his arm.

"I should ask you that," I replied. "Are you really prepared to risk your reputation, because I have no idea about the social mores of the upper classes?"

"Don't worry, all eyes will be on you, but I trust you to be my good girl," he said, winking at me.

"No pressure." I rolled my eyes, and when he looked at me reprovingly, I added a quiet "sir". Sometimes I forgot that he was not only my boss, but also my dom, who remembered my every misstep.

"That wasn't even an insincere apology," he grumbled without losing his smile.

"Sorry, sir." I tried my best to sound as remorseful as possible, so that he wouldn't punish me right then and there. Of course, I loved the way he handled things, but I was going to burst with excitement if I didn't finally enter the gala.

"Better. Still, we'll discuss it in more detail later." He grinned smugly at me and I just managed to restrain myself from rolling my eyes again because I knew exactly how he would discuss it. He, standing, with a smug grin on his face and me, kneeling, naked, and begging for redemption.

Nolan gave me one last dark look before leading me to the main event. Immediately, dozens of pairs of eyes were staring at us, which made me tense up. Everyone wore fine evening dresses, and about three dozen waiters were carrying trays of sparkling wine, champagne, and hor d'oeuvres that were far too pretty to eat in my eyes. The center of the room was used as a dance floor, with a small orchestra playing music in front of it.

I thought the balcony I had been hiding on was huge, but this event set new standards for grand events. The limousines outside had already announced that there was a lot going on here, but it felt like half of New York's high society was here.

The room's ceiling must have been thirty feet high; the west side of the room had a completely glazed wall that offered a fantastic view of the garden. The room was lit by dozens of chandeliers decorated with glass crystals. I immediately heard my grandmother's voice in my head, wondering who was cleaning all the glass.

Nolan skimmed the gathering briefly, then growled softly.

"Typical Bruce and Dylan." He shook his head, and I immediately scanned the room for both of them. I had been so busy with the huge oil paintings and stucco moldings that I had hardly paid any attention to the guests.

Recently, not only Dylan but also Bruce had been visiting Nolan regularly to check on the progress of the merger.

"I don't see them anywhere." The two of them were about the same size as Nolan; when I was in the room with the three men, I always felt as tiny as an ant. Testosterone met mountains of muscle, and shoulders so broad that every woman's heart beat faster.

"That's typical of the two of them," said Nolan. "Dylan never shows up before midnight, and Bruce probably won't show up at all."

We walked along the edge of the dance floor, noticing as we did that conversations between small groups who recognized Nolan kept falling silent when we approached. Excitingly, not a single waiter came to offer us alcohol. Only one waitress, who was handing out orange juice, stopped by briefly.

"So when your business partners aren't there, all the undivided attention is on your shoulders," I said.

"Not quite." He gave me a knowing look. "As promised, everyone's staring at you."

My heart immediately sank into my stomach and I had to control myself not to cover my scars with my other hand. Nolan pulled me tighter against him.

"Do you see? They stare at you because your emerald eyes can dazzle. And if it's not your eyes, it's your smile that catches them." It took a moment, but he was right. I didn't see anyone staring at my scars. "Now that you understand too, your nails could be a little less deep in my arm."

Only now did I realize that I had grabbed onto Nolan's arm. I immediately let go and shook my hands out, whereupon he gave me a smile that made my knees go weak again. He was about to say something when a shrill voice behind me made me flinch.

"Nolan, you look fantastic!" Karen shouted across the dance floor, which she crossed without paying any attention to the dancing guests she ran into. Great.

As usual, she completely ignored me and threw herself so cheaply at Nolan that I almost felt sick.

"Karen," he said briefly, barely glancing at her. "I was just about to lead the most beautiful woman of the evening onto the dance floor." Her eyes began to light up, until Nolan took my hand and looked at me. "Would you do me the honor?"

I nodded, and he led me to the dance floor. If looks could kill... Karen would have done it by now at the latest. Several times in a row.

The orchestra started a new song and I did my best not to look at the edge of the dance floor because Karen was standing there, still piercing me with her angry glares. At least my insecurities were dispelled because Nolan was a gifted dancer who led me to the beat.

"She still wants to kill me, doesn't she?" I asked quietly, to which he laughed. Of all things to elicit a laugh from him, of course it would be a bad joke.

"You're exaggerating," he finally replied in a relaxed manner. He had a good point, but the looks weren't directed at him after all.

"There's no subtle way to give death stares," I pointed out.

"She'll get over it." Maybe he was right. Still, my heart tightened briefly, thinking about how he might dance with another woman someday and think the same about me. Would I get over it? Probably not.

"I wouldn't be so sure," I said, swallowing the lump in my throat.

"Do you want to talk about Karen all evening?" he asked with an undertone that signaled to me that the subject was off the table for him.

"I'm all ears for your suggestions." Shrugging, I let my gaze wander over the part of the dance floor where I knew I wouldn't see Karen.

My arms felt strangely naked, but the great fear that someone would look questioningly at the scars on my arm had not materialized. No one was interested in the traces of my accident. Everyone only had eyes for the fact that I was Nolan Caldwell's escort and being watched in this way somehow felt good. I was proud of the fact that I was his girl.

The orchestra started a slower dance song and I took the opportunity to snuggle even closer to him. I knew that he didn't think much of physical closeness, so I appreciated it all the more that he pulled me even closer to him as he led me across the dance floor.

"Your home is a shithole," Nolan said out of nowhere.

"That's a pretty radical change of subject. And not very flattering either," I muttered dejectedly. I had no idea what he had against my apartment, but he just wouldn't let up on the subject.

"What I meant to say was: you should sleep with me tonight."

It took a second for my brain to process his words. "Why?" I asked, leaning back slightly so that I could look him in the eye.

"Because it's safe with me." He paused meaningfully. "And because you said that pigeons always return to their homes. I want you to always come back to me."

Goosebumps spread up and down my limbs as a million butterflies fluttered around inside me.

"Do I mean anything to you?" I asked, blinking. I had asked him this question before and had never received a satisfactory answer. I hoped from the bottom of my heart that things would be different this time.

"You know the answer," he replied quietly. There was a gentle smile on his lips, but he didn't say what I really wanted to hear. Only if he had said it would it have been real and not wishful thinking.

"I can feel that I mean more to you. But I need to hear it from your mouth." I looked at him expectantly, and he clicked his tongue.

"A sub demands nothing from her dom," he murmured in a serious tone. Of course he blocked it. Typical Nolan. Emotions weren't exactly his strong point, I knew that. That's why I couldn't give up under any circumstances. Not now, when I was so close to being able to look into the depths of his soul.

"I'm not asking for it, I'm asking for it," I replied and smiled at him.

"What do you want to hear from me, little dove?" The hand he'd put around my waist to guide me across the dance floor squeezed me tighter.

"I love you, Nolan," I whispered. "I'd like to hear that the feeling is mutual."

His eyes shone darkly as the words left my mouth. Now it was finally out.

From the first second I scratched his stupid car, I had thought he was the most beautiful man in the world. But I had never thought that I could ever fall in love with Mr. Icecold Heart. Now it had happened and I hoped I hadn't made a mistake in getting involved with him.

"Come to me, little dove. You're mine."

Okay. It wasn't an I love you, but it was pretty close. Close enough for me to get involved.

"But it's in your contract..." I said diplomatically and he interrupted me.

"Fuck the contract," he growled. "Come with me, Blossom. That's not a request, it's an order."

Fuck diplomacy.

Fuck the contract.
Fuck the fear of ending up with a broken heart.

Chapter Eighteen: Let's Deepen the Conversation About Politeness

Nolan

I leaned against the doorframe and watched as Blossom looked around my bedroom.

She was the first woman who had ever made it into my bed. Not only there, but also into the depths of my soul where no woman had ever ventured before.

I don't know how, but she'd effortlessly managed to transform the lump of ice in my chest into a beating heart, which sent a shiver down my spine.

"The starting lineup for the New York Giants could sleep in this bedroom. And the coaches. And their families." She looked at me with wide eyes. "Don't you feel kinda lost and alone in a room this big?"

"I've never felt that way," I answered her, but part of the truth was missing. I had never felt lonely here... until she came into my life.

She had something on the tip of her tongue, but before she could say it, I cut her off.

"Take your clothes off." My command echoed through the room, and the mood immediately changed. She had to swallow her words. Just as well, because I wasn't ready for what she might want to say.

Just the fact that she was here should have shown her clearly enough that she was something special to me. I'd known that from the first second she'd looked at me, with that guilty expression, while her nail polish was eating into the paint on my car. I would have killed anyone else who demolished my car like that... but those eyes.

"Say you're mine," I whispered.

"I'm all yours." Her emerald eyes shone and I nodded in satisfaction. Her response was exactly what this room needed. Her words now hung in the air, and her sweet summer scent would cling to my sheets forever.

Satisfied, I opened the top drawer of the dresser at the other end of the room and took out two leather cuffs, which Blossom looked at with a wry expression. I beckoned her to me with my index finger and she bit her lower lip nervously.

Slowly, so that I could observe her every reaction, I fastened the leather straps around her wrists. A growl escaped my throat as I led her to the wall opposite the bed, where two large carabiners were attached. They were the perfect height for her to stand on tiptoe.

"I thought you didn't like playing games?" she asked. She kept looking above her at her bound hands, which were so far apart that they couldn't touch.

"That's true. But opinions can change." With a shrug, I walked back to the bed and sat down at the foot of it to watch her.

"Some opinions, yes. But your opinions?" She frowned as she shifted her weight on the tips of her toes. I did nothing except leave her alone with her fantasies, but I knew that was enough to make her center throb with desire.

"Do you think I'm conservative?" I countered without answering her question.

"You are the personification of conservative." She grinned at me cheekily, almost provocatively. That's why I took my time with my answer, waiting until she began to breathe heavily with impatience. I enjoyed subtly demonstrating that I had so much power over her.

Fuck. I liked it too much, more than was good for either of us. Why else did I have my entire bedroom remodeled? Because I wanted to dominate her in every way possible, fuck her brains out, and make sure I would be remembered forever.

Maybe it was selfish, but I wanted to make it clear that no other man would ever come close to what I was doing to her. I wanted her to think of me every time she was fucking someone else.

I stood up and walked meaningfully toward her. Each step echoed on the black marble floor, making her flinch slightly each time. Her body was already boiling, asking for more... for everything I could give her.

"I've changed, little dove." My finger ran along her collarbone. "You've changed me."

She smiled softly, but didn't say anything in response, which didn't bother me because there was nothing to say. It was an observation that neither she nor I could change, even if I vehemently denied it in front of Bruce and Dylan.

"And now, let's discuss the subject of politeness in as much detail as you want." The sternness in my tone should have made her shudder, but instead her faint smile turned into a grin.

"That was you, Nolan. You wanted to delve deeper into this topic," she countered.

"You really want to know today?" I whispered.

"Yes, sir." She smiled sweetly at me, and I took that as a challenge, one which I accepted.

How could someone be so innocent, and at the same time the opposite?

I released her from her position and had her kneel down in the middle of the room. After she had braided her hair back, I spread her arms out to the sides so that her palms were facing up. Again, she bit her lower lip expectantly. She still didn't know what was coming, and she thought she was safe. But I knew that in a few minutes she would give me the most sincere apology ever.

Next, I pulled two small but heavy metal balls out of my pocket and dangled them from their connecting cord in front of Blossom's face. The grin slowly disappeared from her face, which made me smile in turn.

"Open your mouth, darling."

She opened her mouth and I slid the love balls into her mouth to moisten them. I left them in her mouth longer than I had to, simply because I could. She had provoked me, and literally begged me to teach her a lesson, so she was going to get a lesson.

My hardness pressed against the fabric of my pants and for a moment I had the insatiable desire to replace the love balls with my manhood, but I held back. First I wanted to hear the most devoted "sir" she could manage.

I got down on my knees in front of her and pressed the love balls against her entrance. She was more than ready for me, and moaned as I pushed the balls into her.

"Don't drop them," I whispered in her ear before getting up again and going back to the dresser. I then lit some candles; they weren't there for decorative reasons, as some might have assumed.

Finally, I took a riding crop out of the drawer and demonstratively stroked Blossom's cheek with the leather tip.

By now she had a love-hate relationship with the crop, of which she made no secret. I loved it when the soft leather left welts on her flawless back, and how her whole body shook under the blows. I could probably bring her to climax with targeted blows alone. But she would have to wait longer for her release today.

"Whose orgasms are yours?" I asked, eager to remind her that she was not allowed to come without my permission.

"You, Nolan." I should correct her for missing a "sir", but the way she pronounced my name... fuck.

I continued to lightly strike her back with the crop until I was sure that I had her undivided attention. Then I turned my attention to her upper arms.

By now, she was no longer hiding the scars on her right arm from me, which made me both happy and stunned at the same time. I was happy because she trusted me so much, and that's exactly what stunned me. I'd never been the kind of man who made commitments. I was so far removed from relationships that it seemed almost impossible to form one. But almost impossible wasn't impossible.

"Move in with me, little dove, and you'll get what you need every night," I whispered seductively. She chewed on her lower lip again.

"That sounds like a promise." She tilted her head and I noticed how her breathing quickened.

"It is. And I'll go even further. You'll not only get what you need, but also what you deserve." That was no longer a promise, but almost a threat, which seemed even more tempting to her.

"I'm starting to get the feeling that this is yet another unfair offer that I can't refuse," she pressed out from behind her pout.

"I never claimed to play fair," I replied with a shrug. It was true, I never had. She had voluntarily entered into a game in which I not only set the rules, but also changed them when I felt like it.

"Touché." She nodded appreciatively at me, but was still far from beaten.

"I won't force you to move in with me, but I might resort to other unfair means to convince you," I said.

"I have no doubt about that, sir." Part of her was reluctant, but I knew she was struggling with herself because she actually wanted to take me up on my offer.

Blossom let her tired arms hang down a little, but I pushed her back up with the tip of the crop.

"Too tired to keep going?" I asked.

"No, sir," she said, trying not to let the effort show.

"Good, then we can carry on with it," I replied with a smile.

"Carry on?" She inhaled heavily before she could control herself again. We both knew the position was getting uncomfortable.

I fetched two thick candles from the dresser and her eyes grew wide.

"You want me to hold still again, don't you?" She seemed to remember our first night together just as well as I did. That night had burned itself into my brain, and I was aware that I couldn't erase everything associated with it from my mind.

"No," I replied curtly.

"No?" She frowned and gave me a questioning look.

"It would be in your own interest not to move, but this time it's not an order." I placed the two candles on her palms and watched in amusement as she realized the game. Every time she moved her arms, a little wax dripped down onto her sensitive skin.

"Easy-peasy," she muttered, strain in her voice. Damn, I just loved humiliating her even further for her defiant reactions.

"In that case..." I didn't finish the sentence, but silently picked up the two more candles, which I placed on her forearms.

"Still easy-peasy?"

She bit her lips as I used her own words against her. She took a deep breath, but then slowed down and put on a diplomatic face. "I'd say it's appropriately stressful."

"Well saved, little dove." Otherwise I would have had a whole arsenal of candles and other things to drive her mad.

"Thank you, sir." Slowly her defiance faded; now she was ready to give herself to me completely.

I watched with satisfaction as she found it increasingly difficult to keep her arms up. The candles were designed to be balanced on a person's arms, but it almost looked like a work of art, how Blossom was reflected in the candlelight on the polished marble floor.

"Are you still okay?" I asked, my sympathetic expression a sharp contrast to my dominant posture.

"Yes, sir." She nodded, even though her arms began to tremble.

"Good girl." I let the tip of the crop wander over her body. "Don't let anything fall down."

"No, sir."

"I expect you to say when you've reached your limit." I looked at her insistently and deliberately chose a stern, almost reprimanding tone of voice.

She nodded again, then concentrated on her breathing and posture.

Her legs trembled more with each passing minute and I knew that the love balls were getting to her. Not much longer and the toy would force her to orgasm. Together with the tension, the heat of the candles, and the tickle of my breath on her skin.

She held on bravely, and only when she had really reached her limit did she blink at me.

"I can't go on any longer," she whispered, exhausted. She was close to her limit, but I know that she could go further

"You can go longer," I said, but I took the candles off her right arm. "Keep your arms up." I took the rest of the candles off, growling with satisfaction as she fought the urge to let her arms go.

"Please, sir!" she begged, allowing her arms to tremble. Now that the candles were gone, there was no reason for her to stay still.

"Are you sorry?" I asked, and she nodded so vigorously that a few strands of hair came loose from her braid.

"Yes, sir!" Her tone signaled to me that she was not only at the end, but wanted more at the same time. She wanted to be fucked, hard and deep and to the point of unconsciousness.

"What are you sorry for?" I asked.

"Everything!" she blurted out. A simple answer, one that I wasn't satisfied with.

"You can do better than that, little dove. What am I punishing you for right now?" I tapped her chin with the crop and forced her to look me in the eye again. Her whole body shook; she was on the verge of coming. The love balls seemed to massage her perfectly.

"Earlier, at the gala! I only apologized half-heartedly," she replied after a moment's thought. Her head must have been spinning from all the input. The pain, the lust, my bedroom, it all had to be overwhelming her right now.

"So, what do I expect from you now?" I looked at her expectantly.

"An apology?" She bit her lips together and suppressed a gasp; her arms must be burning like hell.

"Was that a question or a statement?" Fuck. I liked this too much; I wanted to drag it out as much as possible.

"An observation, sir! I'm sorry!" At first her answers had been a whisper, now she was almost shouting at me. "Really, sir! I'm very sorry!"

"Hmm." I walked around her while I let her words sink in.

"I don't think I've ever regretted a sentence as much as I did just now."

"I think so too." I grazed her lower lip with my thumb and she willingly opened her mouth. Then I placed the crop between her lips and put my hands in my pants pockets with a grin. Blossom was practically exploding with frustration because I still hadn't released her.

She didn't say it out loud, but it was exactly the things she idolized me for: when I showed her how depraved she was because she liked being humiliated by me. I didn't have to look to know how wet she was getting for me.

"You can relax," I finally said.

"Thank you, sir." At the same moment, her arms dropped down and she sank lower to her knees as her upper body also gave way and her shoulders fell forward. She sighed gratefully as I took the love balls out of her dripping core and put them to one side.

Because her muscles were still trembling, I carried her to bed. She needed her release. And I needed her release even more.

In bed, I secured her arms to more carabiners attached to either side of the headboard, which elicited a frustrated gasp from her.

"I'm beginning to hate your bedroom," she replied, blowing a strand of hair out of her face.

"The chances of not being tied up here would increase if you moved in with me," I replied coolly. I tried not to make a big deal out of it, but the deal was pretty damn big.

Blossom was the first woman I wanted to be around... no, needed to be around. Just the thought of her living in that dump of an apartment every day, and having no sense of the danger of her neighborhood, made my muscles tense.

"Nolan..." she began, tilting her head. I knew she was about to refuse me, so I unzipped my pants and sank my hardness so deep inside her that the rest of her words faded into a moan.

I fucked every ounce of sense that she possessed out of her body.

"You're staying here tonight," I whispered in her ear, to which she nodded.

"Yes, sir."

I grabbed her hips and thrust harder. I wanted her to feel, with every fiber of her body, that she belonged to me.

"That's you, my good girl." It wasn't forever, but tonight was enough for me for now. "Come for me."

She tightened around me, so tightly that I gave in to the pressure and came. Her sweet moans echoed through the room, slowly fading into soft whimpers. I enjoyed the waves of her climax for a moment, then rolled to the side and lay down next to her. I closed my eyes.

"Haven't you forgotten something?" she asked, shaking the leather cuffs so that they jingled softly.

"No. But you are," I replied, folding my hands on my stomach.

"Thank you, sir," she mumbled, making no secret of the fact that she didn't like my answer.

"What lesson have we just learned?" I raised a brow and she gasped.

"Pleasantries, sir." She put on a serious face again and bit the insides of her cheeks hard enough for me to see.

"Do you need a refresher?" I asked provocatively. I admit, I wouldn't have minded fucking her again on the spot.

"No, sir! No more today." Her irregular breathing made it clear to me that she'd really had enough. At least for tonight.

"Good." I turned my gaze away from her and stared at the ceiling.

Blossom punished me with fiery glances for a few more minutes, all of which I enjoyed, before she fell asleep.

I was supposed to sleep too, but I couldn't manage more than a restless doze because I was too agitated. I liked the idea that she could always sleep in my bed. At the same time, the thought of her not doing so at some point killed me. No one could guarantee that she wouldn't simply disappear as soon as she had paid off her debt.

Every bird flies away at some point...

Ironically, the weather outside mirrored my inner emotional world. The heavy, black clouds were packed tightly together, and the air crackled more and more. All hell was bound to break loose out there any second.

At least that's what the rumbling thunder announced.

Chapter Nineteen: Florida Road

Nolan

I rolled to one side on the soft mattress and continued watching Blossom sleep. At first her sleep was calm and deep, even though she was still bound to the bed by her wrists.

But as the weather grew darker, she became increasingly restless.

The storm had drawn closer and every streak of lightning that flashed through the dark night sky was followed by a deep rumble of thunder.

At some point, she started mumbling unintelligible things that I couldn't decipher. I didn't understand anything except two words.

Florida Road.

She had never used her safeword, but it was still like a punch in the gut to hear it out loud.

Her breathing was irregular and her body began to tremble. And me? I felt more helpless than ever, because I didn't know how to help her. So I did the only thing I could think of. I pulled her as tightly as I could and whispered soothing words in her ear.

Slowly, her body relaxed, but when a booming clap of thunder echoed through the dark night sky, startling even me, she startled as far up as her restraints would allow.

"Not Florida Road!" she yelled, before blinking in confusion and looking around.

"It's okay, little dove, it was just a dream." I ran a hand through her hair and hugged her tighter to me.

"I know," she replied breathlessly. "But it still feels like I'm back in that night."

"I know," I echoed her words, and she looked at me as if I didn't know anything. But I understood her nightmares better than she realized.

I took her hand and placed it on my torso. "Three broken ribs." Then I moved my hand further. up "This collarbone, twice, within three months... my left arm was only broken once, but it was dislocated twice. There are no scars, but I feel the pain every day. Every morning when I drink a glass of bourbon, I tell myself not to be like him."

I paused to swallow down the burgeoning anger that rose up in me every time I thought of my maker. Ironically, the most effective way to get rid of him was a good sparring session at Left Hook Haven.

Blossom's eyes grew wide. "You haven't had any bourbon the last few days."

"I know," I replied proudly. Since I had given her the dress for the gala, I hadn't touched a drop of alcohol. I didn't have to demonstrate to my messed-up family in any other way that I wasn't like them. I no longer had to prove anything to anyone.

"Why not?" she asked cautiously, her gaze saying that she was curious but didn't want to offend me.

"That's the wrong question. You should be asking why this morning bourbon ritual came about in the first place," I replied as I untied her so she could get a better look at me.

"Why?" She rubbed her wrists. The leather cuffs had left slight marks on her skin that would disappear in a few minutes.

"My father was an alcoholic. The bad kind. So bad that my mother left when I was young that I can't even remember her face," I started to explain, but then faltered because Blossom opened her mouth to say something.

"I'm so sorry," she whispered sincerely. She felt bad about what had happened to me. Why? Because she was too good for this goddamn world.

"Don't be, it's not your fault." I took a deep breath and let new air fill my lungs. "I've been drinking bourbon every morning since my twenty-first birthday, just to prove to myself that I could stop anytime I wanted to. Every morning I remind myself not to become like him, despite the genes I can't change." I rubbed at the skin of my arm, as if I could simply scrape off the genes I shared with my parents.

"I don't know your father, but I know you're a good person." She said this so convincingly that I felt sick. I wasn't a good person, but she was right about one thing.

"You've made me a better person," I said in a hoarse voice; a part of me couldn't believe it myself.

"Why are you telling me this?" She looked at me curiously.

"Because you helped me, little dove. And now I want to help you." I got out of bed and grabbed her hand so that she would follow me.

The marble floor felt cold under my bare feet. I buttoned my pants and tossed my shirt to Blossom, because she wasn't wearing anything else.

She flinched at every clap of thunder until we arrived in the living room.

"Wow," she whispered when she saw the huge grand piano that was the center of the room. "That looks like a Steinway."

She looked as though she hardly dared to approach the piano, for fear of breaking it with her mere presence.

"That's a Steinway. From Hamburg, to be precise," I confirmed her assumption.

She looked at me with a quirked brow. "You know that Steinway & Sons also have a factory in New York?"

Her question made me grin. I had recently acquired more knowledge about grand pianos than most music students.

"Yes, but you probably also know that the instruments made in Hamburg are the better ones," I pointed out.

Blossom gasped. "You're crazy." Stunned, she stepped closer to the piano, but still didn't touch it.

"Crazy about you," I replied.

"But mostly crazy." She exhaled, trying to hide her flushed cheeks; my gift had embarrassed her, even though there was no reason for it.

"My car had to be brought here from Europe anyway, and because there was still room..." With a shrug, I tapped on the varnished wood of the lid.

"So it was totally self-serving?" She frowned because she didn't quite believe me.

"You could say that." My dry tone elicited a smile from her.

"Thank you." Her eyes shone brighter than ever before, and that alone had made all the effort worthwhile.

"The feeling is mutual. You helped me, and now I'm helping you."

The next boom of thunder made her jolt, and I pointed to the leather seat in front of the ivory keys.

"Play for me, little dove," I urged her.

She hesitantly took a seat and let her fingers glide over the keys without eliciting a sound from the piano.

"What do you want me to play for you?" She took her fingers off the ivories and fiddled with the hem of my shirt, which only half-heartedly covered her body. It was storming outside, but the air in here was so oppressive and hot that it was almost unbearable.

"Whatever's on your mind," I replied. At the Royal Red, she had played most of her own songs, and proved that she would have been a great pianist if fate hadn't had its own plans. Fate was sometimes a whore, but if you had a strong will and more money than Midas, you could fight fate yourself—and I was ready for that.

"Hmmm," she murmured. She paused, then thoughtfully hit the first key. Within a few seconds, she was completely immersed in the notes as her fingers flew across the keys. The storm continued to rage around us, but Blossom relaxed more and more.

"It works..." she mumbled, stunned. "How did you know it would work?"

"I didn't know," I confessed honestly. "But I hoped it would help you."

I loved the unique way her eyes sparkled when she played, and how she lost herself completely in the sound of her melodies. When she played, all her fears left her body.

"I've never spoken to anyone about the accident, not even during therapy," she said, as if out of nowhere.

"You don't have to talk about it now," I replied.

"You already know what happened anyway, don't you?"

I didn't answer. Of course, I had had her entire life investigated. But that had happened long before I had developed feelings for her. Blossom took my silence as a yes.

"Then I don't have to explain that those idiots completely overestimated themselves. Or that they left me in the car, and I had to break a window to free myself." Her right hand tensed briefly, but she carried on playing. "I have no idea what happened to everyone, but to be honest, I don't really care. It can't be helped that they destroyed my future."

I found it remarkable how determined she was to put her past behind her. In that respect, she had more strength than I would ever have. I still hadn't forgiven my father for anything.

"All doors are open to you, Blossom," I said sincerely, because that's exactly what I meant.

"That's not true, but thank you." She forced a pained smile before concentrating on the music again.

"My door is open to you, and so is the rest of the world," I explained matter-of-factly, because it was the most normal thing in the world for me. Sometimes I forgot that the world looked different from the executive floor of Caldwell Tower than it did from further down.

"I don't need the rest of the world." She waved a hand, but faltered briefly. "But…"

"But?" I asked when I realized that she was caught up in her thoughts.

"Your door sounds pretty tempting. And to come back to your question from earlier, yes. I want to move in with you. On one condition." She looked at me meaningfully.

"And that would be?" I asked, still in disbelief that she had agreed to move in with me.

"Miss Scratchy comes too, and she sleeps in the bed. That's if she doesn't sulk for the next few weeks because I'm not coming home tonight." She rolled her eyes and giggled at the same time.

The storm slowly subsided, but we still didn't move. She began a new song, and I watched with fascination at how sensitively she played.

There was more feeling than I was ever able to feel… or give.

Without a doubt, I had given Blossom everything I could give her, but at the same time I wondered if it was enough.

Chapter Twenty: You're Literally Begging For a Challenge

Blossom

Had I been naive when I believed that something would change after I moved in with Nolan?

And how. In the office, he was still the worst boss in the world, which I somehow found secretly sexy. Especially now that I knew I meant more to him than he showed on the outside.

For someone like Nolan Caldwell, letting someone into his apartment was a huge deal, so I was all the more proud that I had even made it into his bed... when I wasn't kneeling in front of it.

Nevertheless, this led me to make ambitious plans. First I conquered his bed, and then his heart.

Because I'd already done my morning tasks, there was nothing for me to do but rest my head on my hands, stare languidly in the direction of Nolan's office, and occasionally reply to Ruby's texts.

"Blossom." I could hear his serious tone even through the noise of the intercom that connected our desks.

"I'm coming, sir," I replied and set off straight away.

"What is it?" I asked curiously as I opened his door a crack.

"The documents for the presentation, please." He didn't look up from his desk. "And please bring me the papers from the copy room."

I immediately dashed off to fetch the documents I had been working meticulously on for the last few days. I had checked every figure three times, and carefully gone over all the data, because I wanted to do a perfect job.

I almost forgot the papers from the copy room, though. Nolan was one of the few people who insisted on not having a printer in his office.

Smiling, I heard his voice in my head as he gave me a short lecture on how inefficient an office printer was because it made noise, because the printer ink stank, and how he also rather liked bossing me around.

I headed quickly to the copy room, which was not a small room smelling of printer's ink and stale filter coffee, but a huge room with floor-to-ceiling windows, a seating area with leather armchairs, and a giant TV. It was bigger than my old apartment.

On the way back, I almost collided with Karen, who was skulking around outside Nolan's office as if she had something on her mind.

When she saw me, she flinched like a startled cat, only to immediately extend her claws.

"What are you doing here?" she asked in a waspish tone.

"Work," I replied shortly. I'd really perfected that tone of voice since I'd known Nolan, because I'd learned from the best. "I should probably ask you what you're doing here."

She wrinkled her nose. "I work here too."

I glanced at the clock hanging above my desk.

"The presentation isn't for over an hour. Or did Dylan get here earlier?" I looked around but couldn't see him anywhere.

"I'm here early to make sure everything is perfect."

She was more likely here to make sure she had enough time to give Nolan plenty of fuck-me looks. I suppressed the urge to roll my eyes.

"Whatever," I muttered. I was about to walk past her when she grabbed my arm and stopped me.

"Sooner or later, he will get fed up with you and throw you out of his office."

"Maybe," I replied with a disinterested shrug. His car was parked in his company parking lot, looking like new, and my debts were almost paid off. So there was no real reason to work here anymore.

"You don't seem to care much about him," Karen said, pulling the corners of her mouth down in disdain.

"If he kicks me out of the office, I'll just wait in our apartment for him to finish work."

She inhaled sharply. "What?"

"That's right, I'm staying with Nolan. He asked me and I said yes. Without any contracts."

Yes, there was perhaps a little too much pride in my voice, but I couldn't help but rub Karen's nose in it. I could finally pay her back for all the nasty looks she gave me at every single meeting, and it worked.

She was clearly boiling with rage, and barely managing to suppress her emotions. But suddenly her facial expression changed and a shiver went down my spine.

"We didn't need a contract for our fuck either," she replied, razor-sharp, giving me a death stare. "And that's exactly why you should be prepared for him to come back to me."

She put her hands on her hips and I buried myself behind the papers I was supposed to take to Nolan. I shouldn't let her get me down, but her concentrated viciousness made me swallow hard.

"You're telling me that Mr. 'I-need-a-contract-for-everything' didn't want to draw up a contract?" I asked, frowning.

Ever since I'd known Nolan, he'd demanded a written contract for every little obligation. Even if he was just having a four dollar cup of coffee at Daisy's, he would demand the receipt.

"Exactly, that's what I said. Are you deaf, or just stupid?"

Okay, now Karen was pushing my buttons. I scraped together all the restraint I could muster not to stick it to her. In situations like this, I wished I was blessed with Ruby's self-confidence. If she were me, she would have immediately known how to send this bitch running with a few harsh words.

"That's a lie," I said, trying not to look as insecure as I felt at the moment.

"A lie? I don't need to lie about it. But if it makes you feel better, believe what you want." She waved her hand meaningfully in the air.

She had every reason to lie, and it would suit her personality, but the thought that it could be the truth, even if the odds were one in a hundred thousand, gave my heart a little twinge.

"Now if you'll excuse me, I have work to do," I said, squeezing past her.

When I got to Nolan's office I slammed the door behind me, which earned me an irritated look from him.

"Whoops," I whispered, smiling apologetically. "Karen's out there."

"What is she doing outside my office?" he asked, sighing softly.

"I don't have a clue, but I'm sure she'll enlighten us in a minute." I rolled my eyes, making no secret of the fact that I didn't like her.

"Is it true that you two..." I faltered before I could finish the sentence.

"What makes you think that?" He looked at me calmly, his expression neutral. He made it impossible for me to figure out what was going on inside him. His poker face was just too good for me.

"I don't know. You could call it female intuition."

"Female intuition?"

"Or maybe she claimed you slept with her. Without a contract, mind you." I grinned awkwardly. "But that would be ridiculous."

He remained silent, which was not a good sign at all.

"Or?" I asked.

But before he could answer, the door swung open and Dylan and Bruce stormed into the office, closely followed by Karen. She stopped at the doorway and showed off her curves, stomping around on her Louboutins.

I wasn't supposed to think that maybe there really had been more between Nolan and her, but I couldn't help it. Karen was literally forcing the whole world to watch her try to seduce him by any means necessary.

I anxiously pulled the sleeves of my button-up blouse further over my wrists, as I always did when I was nervous.

"You're early," said Nolan, but to my surprise he didn't sound angry. He usually hated it when people stormed into his office, and even more when they stormed in ahead of schedule.

"Well, the problems are forcing us to act," Dylan replied. "Hey, kiddo." He winked at me and I smiled back.

"Minor problems." Nolan waved a dismissive hand.

"But still, problems." Bruce's deep tone echoed through the room. As always when the three of them were together, I felt dizzy; so much concentrated testosterone in such a small space simply couldn't be good.

"Are the documents ready?" Nolan asked me.

I nodded. "Yes, sir, double-checked and printed in triplicate," I replied instantly, as if shot from a pistol.

He stood up and pointed to the door. "Go to the briefing room, I'll be right there."

I wanted to go ahead, to show his business partners around the executive floor, which they probably knew better than I did, but he clicked his tongue.

"You stay here, Blossom. Karen can lead them there, she knows the floor."

"Of course, sir." I tried to keep calm, but after the excitement with Karen, I found it difficult; I knew exactly why he was keeping me here. He wanted to check my work a third time. I hadn't made a single misstep since my first day at work, and had organized everything carefully. Apart from his extra sandwich requests, which changed depending on his mood and was the reason why only psychics could order the right things at Daisy's, I was doing an almost perfect job.

After Karen had left the office in slow motion and closed the door behind her, I took a deep breath to lecture Nolan on how there was no reason not to trust me. Especially since we even slept in the same bed, which required basic trust. At least for me.

But instead of letting me talk, he pulled me close and robbed me of any basis for discussion with a deep and passionate kiss. His hand slipped between my legs and he murmured against my lips as he massaged my most sensitive spot, feeling how hot it made me.

"You wanted to say something?" he asked with a grin. His hands wandered down my body; he grabbed my braid, forcing me to tilt my head back. I loved it when he did that. When he dominated me, but was so tender at the same time, I wanted to cry with joy.

"Not anymore," I replied, gasping. He drove me crazy within seconds and I was powerless against it.

"Out with it, little dove." He looked at me gloomily and I shook my head once more.

"Not important, sir." It really wasn't important. All that mattered were his hands on my body.

"You thought I was checking your work." It wasn't a question, but a statement, and his serious look signaled to me that he was sure.

"My impeccable work, mind you," I corrected him. If I had already lost, then I might as well go down in a blaze of glory.

"Flawless then? That calls for a challenge," he whispered seductively.

"Go ahead, I've been working on these papers for weeks, I know them inside out. There's not a single mistake." I put my hands on my hips and straightened my shoulders. He couldn't unsettle me in that respect. My work was flawless, I was convinced of that.

"You know them by heart?" He raised a brow, which made me weak in the knees; he always looked good enough to eat.

"Yes, sir." I grinned provocatively at him.

"In that case..." He didn't finish his sentence. The next moment, something small and cool entered me, making me groan.

Oh God. The love balls again? No. It was far too easy for that. The next moment he pushed my skirt back into place and smoothed everything out.

"Come on, the others are waiting." He gave me a pat on the bottom, then opened the door for me.

I grabbed the documents and followed him. When I got to the meeting room, I was still reeling from his kiss, and whatever was inside me.

Nolan threw himself onto the free leather chair at the head of the table, then put his feet up and pointed at me.

"My lovely assistant will present the quarterly accounts and everything we have planned for the next three months."

I nodded with a smile, because his words hadn't quite reached me. I handed out the documents, and only then did the penny drop.

I was to give the presentation. Not only in front of his business partners, who were like a part of his family, but also in front of Karen, plus a few other nameless faces that I only knew by sight.

"Are you sure, sir?" I asked cautiously as I handed over all the documents.

"That shouldn't be a problem for you, since you've prepared everything." He put one hand in his pocket and the next moment I felt a vibration. Inside me.

Good God.

"Easypeasy," I said in a strained voice. Immediately, there was a response as the vibrations got stronger. I refrained from cursing Nolan, because he looked at me every time I did it. I had no idea how many vibration levels the device had, but I wasn't eager to find out.

So I gritted my teeth and did my best. But the best wasn't good enough for him. Or at least, not as entertaining as he had imagined, because he continued to increase the vibration at regular intervals.

I would have liked to bite the inside of my cheeks, hard, but I couldn't speak like that, so I disguised my panting with a coughing fit.

"Are you okay?" Dylan asked as I coughed again. I knew Nolan was about to kick it up a notch.

"Everything's fine," I managed. "Must be the pollen." I whirled my hands through the air to imitate a pollen flight.

Nolan leaned back with a grin. From the smug smile on his face, he was clearly enjoying himself as I tried not to make a fool of myself. I kept giving him looks that made it clear how much I hated him for doing this, but I couldn't really blame him.

At least there was one good thing about it, it took my mind off Karen and what exactly had happened between them. I didn't get the feeling that Nolan was interested in her, but most people probably felt the same way about me.

To be honest, I had felt like something special when he said that he would have fucked me even if I hadn't signed the contract back then. To my ears, it had sounded like that had never happened before.

As I stared out of the window for longer than was appropriate for a lecture, Nolan cleared his throat and stared at me seriously.

"Focus, Blossom."

I took a deep breath and tried to ignore the fact that he was driving me crazy. He owed me at least two orgasms tonight for this. Maybe even three.

After an interminably long time, I finished my presentation. Afterward, Dylan and Bruce immediately got into a heated discussion, because they were sitting opposite each other and had very different personalities.

In the past, I would never have believed that there were several versions of the "man-with-broad-shoulders-and-gloomy-eyes" type, but today I only had to look at the three men to know it was true.

"Calm down, we're not at the Haven," Nolan growled as Dylan slapped the table with the flat of his hand.

"Maybe we should discuss it further there?" Dylan suggested.

"We would agree on that," Bruce replied.

"Do you actually listen to yourselves?" Shaking his head, Nolan stood up and rubbed his temples. He pointed at the men from the board, whom I didn't know. "Out."

Everyone immediately jumped up at once, leaving only Karen, me, and concentrated testosterone behind.

"You too," Nolan continued, pointing at Karen and me. "We have something to talk about."

As I got ready to leave the room without hesitation, he held out his notes for me to copy. He grabbed my wrist and pulled me down to him.

"Don't forget where we left off, little dove. I'm going to pick up later." He glared at me darkly.

"Yes, sir," I breathed back, because I couldn't manage any more. "After the break?"

"There's no break." He grinned darkly at me as I realized I had to somehow endure the vibrator until he, Dylan, and Bruce were done with their argument.

Oh God. Oh God. Oh God.

Chapter Twenty-One: The Whole World is Unfair

Blossom

Waiting outside the door for Nolan was the worst thing I could have imagined. I wanted to run home and hide under the covers with Little Miss Scratchy.

The situation called for a cozy *Gilmore Girls* marathon and a family-sized stash of Ben & Jerry's.

At least I didn't have to deal with Karen's death stares, because she had marched straight out of the executive floor. During the conference, her snide looks had almost thrown me off my game time and again.

To make matters worse, the device inside me vibrated on and on and on. It wasn't long before I had an orgasm in front of the whole team... or maybe not.

Because suddenly the vibrator stopped, and I breathed out and finally relaxed. Perhaps Nolan wasn't the bastard I thought he was after all.

None of the board members he had thrown out of the room said a word, and I remained quiet until the silence became suffocating. Then Karen came back, grinning like the Grinch at a catastrophic Christmas disaster.

The longer I watched her, the more certain I became that she was up to something. I had no idea what she was plotting this time, but my bad gut feeling wouldn't be fooled. Something was up.

She stared confidently at the door, ready to pounce on anyone who left the entrance area. Not a good sign. I reminded myself all the more to keep calm, because I didn't want to be thrown off course by this woman.

When the three men finally left the conference room, they all had such fixed expressions on their faces that I had no idea whether they had come to an agreement. The three of them playing poker had to be a real challenge, or a very expensive lesson.

"You can go, the documents will be sent out this afternoon," Nolan said to the board as we walked past. I immediately caught up with him.

Karen trotted along as well, to my irritation, going up to Dylan and linking arms with him.

"How did it go?" I asked quietly. After all, there was a small chance that there was only a discussion because of me, because I hadn't presented the figures with the same aplomb as Nolan.

"Good," he said curtly, then fell silent again; the walk to his office suddenly seemed endless.

"Oh, of course. How could I have misinterpreted your beaming faces?" I replied with a grin.

"You're joking," he replied dryly, without looking at me. He really was a tough nut to crack again today.

"Yep. And you should have been grinning." I nodded to emphasize my point.

"Later," he replied and waved me off. He was typical Mr. Icecold again, but I grinned to myself because the Nolan of this morning had been a different one—the kiss-me-on-the-forehead guy who had brought me coffee in bed and carried Miss Scratchy around in his arms like a supervillain.

"That's not how humor works," I muttered. "Thanks, by the way."

"For what?" He stopped, irritated, and put his hands in his pockets. Now I finally had his full attention, but judging by the look on his face, I was only partially pleased.

"For the break," I replied with a shrug, doing my best not to look as guilty as I felt. Not that I was guilty of anything, but he was good at making me think I was.

Nolan raised a brow in surprise as he looked me up and down. He lingered on my no longer vibrating but still throbbing center.

"Remind me to buy something with better batteries next time."

"Yes, sir." I bit my lips. So he hadn't been my hero in shining armor after all; it was the weak batteries I had to thank.

Behind me, Karen caught my attention when she threw herself at Dylan.

"Tell me, boss," she began. Out of the corner of my eye, I saw him trying to shake her off like an annoying fly, but he failed. "There are still so many documents to get. And while I'm here, wouldn't it make sense for me to stay here and pick them up directly from the various departments, instead of waiting for them to be faxed or mailed at some point?"

I tensed up when I saw Dylan's reaction; my muscles went bone hard.

"Sounds like a good plan, actually. I've been waiting three days for the reports from the finance department."

"Good, then I'll stay here and go back to Mercer Solutions with Nolan later."

I cleared my throat, barely managing to swallow the words that were on the tip of my tongue.

Karen gave me a smug look. "What? I thought you were riding your little scooter as usual."

"It's a Honda," I said calmly, biting my tongue. Insulting me was one thing, but labeling my bike as a scooter was a bit too derogatory.

"Whatever." She waved her hand in the air as we reached Nolan's office. "Anyway, I think it's nice that Nolan has his racing car back. It suits him much better than that black, characterless Porsche."

Dylan looked curiously at Nolan. "Your Maserati is back?"

"A few days already," he replied, coolly pointing to the key lying on his table as if it was no big deal. Having a car flown to Europe to be painted there was probably no big deal for billionaires.

"And you didn't mention it at all?" Dylan followed up.

"No big deal." He took the words out of my mouth, but Dylan's reaction proved my theory wrong.

"Did you hear that, Bruce? No big deal, he says." Shaking his head, Dylan grabbed a glass and poured himself a bourbon.

"I heard it," Bruce replied, pouring a drink and taking a sip. They both looked at each other meaningfully. They almost acted as if Nolan had a real obsession with the car. Maybe that was true, because I'd never seen him drive it, apart from the time I'd shot the paintwork.

I swallowed as I realized how important the car must be to him, and what I had done with it.

"I've had it brought to the garage, but I haven't driven it yet," Nolan finally said.

Dylan and Bruce looked at him with equal irritation, which was another indication that he liked his car more than I had thought.

"So you're not going to take the Maserati?" Karen sounded more disappointed than was appropriate.

"Probably not," he replied coolly, already poring over the next documents.

"But you should! Absolutely! We'd get to Dylan much quicker." Her voice was a little hoarse, and a knot formed in my stomach at the thought of him actually taking her in his car while I was literally the fifth wheel with my Honda.

"We'll see then." With that, Nolan cut her off for good and turned his attention to his emails.

"Well, I'm going to get to work," Karen said excitedly, rubbing her hands together. I noticed that she had a black mark on her hand that hadn't been there this morning.

"You've got something there." I pointed to the stain, foreseeing the drama of black marks on important documents and who was to blame. She stared at the stain for a moment, gasped, and then waved me off.

"Just some makeup." She trotted off in her heels, like in a bad dance movie.

Dylan rolled his eyes. "Just some makeup. Probably the oil change collection from Lé Werkstatt," he said with a grin. I stifled a giggle.

Then he and Bruce also retreated, ostensibly to have a coffee at Daisy's. But the unofficial version, which everyone in the office knew, was that they were taking a smoke break on the roof of Caldwell Industries. After heated conversations, Bruce often went out for a smoke, even when we were at Mercer Solutions.

I hadn't been to Dylan's company building often, but I liked it there. A huge skyscraper at the other end of Central Park, it was at least as impressive as Caldwell Industries. Just thinking about this afternoon made me feel sick to my stomach.

Only when I was sure that everyone was out of earshot did I clear my throat.

"You don't really want to go to Mercer Solutions alone with Karen, do you?" My voice shook; I couldn't make a secret of my insecurity. Insecurity mixed with jealousy really brought out the worst in me.

"Not particularly. But what would be so bad about it?" Nolan didn't even bother to look at me. There seemed to be absolutely no problem for him.

"You don't see what I would find bad about that?" I gave him a reproachful look, which bounced off him.

I felt like tearing my hair out. Most of the time I didn't mind his cold demeanor, because I knew he was capable of feeling something. But in situations like this, his non-reaction didn't make my self-doubt any better.

"No, I don't know what's so wrong about it." He still didn't look at me, but continued with his work.

"Come on. Even you can't be so cold that you don't realize how much Karen makes me uncomfortable." I leaned against the desk, hoping my gesture would get more attention and it worked. He looked up from his work with a sigh.

"There's no reason for your insecurity," he said. His words reassured me somewhat. To be honest, I'd never had the feeling that he was remotely interested in Karen, but I also knew that perseverance, curves, and stiletto Louboutins could still go a long way.

"Really?" I asked, blinking.

"I've decided for you." He said it as simply as if we had been talking about the weather, the evening news, or a bland meal.

"I know. But *she* doesn't know," I pointed out.

"Which doesn't matter to either you or me," he replied, folding his hands on the desk. A sign that the subject was over for him. I should let it go too, but I couldn't let the subject go just yet. Not until all doubts had been dispelled.

I took a deep breath. "She doesn't give you horrible looks all the time. Or tell you lies. I mean, what are the chances that you two have been fucking without a contract?"

"Oh, Blossom. Just let it go." He exhaled heavily, which made me angry. Didn't he realize how much this issue was bothering me? And didn't he realize that his answer wasn't really an answer?

"You didn't deny it," I replied, frowning.

"No." That was all he said. And that was exactly what made my pulse shoot up to an unhealthily high level.

"So it's true?" I held my breath and thought I could hear my heart breaking quietly in the distance.

"It didn't mean anything," he replied emphatically, but that couldn't stop the avalanche of feelings he had unleashed in me.

"Good God, it is true," I whispered, feeling completely powerless. Half of New York must have just heard my heart shatter into a thousand pieces.

"Again, it was so meaningless to me that I didn't need a contract." Nolan propped his elbows on the desk and gave me a stern "hold-your-tongue" look, but I didn't think to shut up now. If anything needed to be said between us, it was this.

"Is that what you told her? That she meant nothing to you? Or did she say no when you stood on her doorstep, like you did with me back then, and that's why you fucked her without a contract?" Tears burned behind my eyelids, but I fought them bravely, no matter how much it hurt.

He rolled his eyes. He had just made my dreams collapse like a house of cards, with the force of a hurricane, and he had the nerve to roll his eyes. I was stunned and couldn't think straight.

"What do you want to hear from me now, Blossom?" He clenched his jaw, gazing at me like I was a business partner who wanted to change the terms of the contract. Yet my heart was more than just an annoying bargaining chip. It was all I had.

"I thought I was special to you," I breathed, shaking my head. I still couldn't believe we were having this discussion.

"You are something special. You mean something to me." His voice softened. I was on the verge of believing him. At least I didn't hear a lie, but what did that mean? He had also claimed that he needed a contract for everything.

"Then why do you only show it so rarely?" I asked, confused.

"You know it's not easy for me," he replied, dropping his gaze.

"It's not easy for me either, but I still show my feelings. But you don't show it, most of the time you don't even say anything." I confronted him with the bare facts, but they bounced off him without leaving a scratch.

"What more proof do you want from me?" He stood up from his desk and straightened his shoulders as if he were about to go on the attack. "Do you want me to marry you first, to prove to you that I care about you? Fine, let's get married. Right now if you like." He pointed to the door and my jaw dropped.

"Are any of these other women still in your life? No!" I said, practically shouting.

"Why do you refuse if it's so important to you?" He looked at me as if I'd lost my mind. But it was him who was talking crazy.

"Because it's a big deal to me! You don't propose on the spur of the moment. You plan everything meticulously. And in the meantime, you go through all the dreams that have accumulated over time, and you listen to yourself to see which ones cause the biggest tingling in your stomach. It makes a big difference whether you get married in a blooming lavender field, or at sunset on a powdered sugar beach. Or by lovelessly signing a piece of soulless paper just because you've had an argument."

"Unlike you, I've been busy with other things most of my life," Nolan growled. He hadn't talked much about his past, but I knew he had worked for everything he had today.

"That's unfair," I replied. We all had our own strategies for dealing with the past. His method had worked better for him in some respects. But at what cost? There was no heart beating in his chest, just an ice-cold lump that twitched from time to time.

"The whole world is unfair. Get over it, little dove," he replied pessimistically.

I stared at him in disbelief. Did he really just say that?

"Assuming I get over the unfair world, would you be able to love me?" I put my hands on my hips and waited for him to finally let his feelings out. But instead he just stared at me angrily and sat back in his chair.

"We'll see when the time comes." He went back to his work. I was about to explode.

Streptopelia turtur. Columba livia. Streptopelia decaocto.

And that was my cue. At first I had wanted to run away, as I always did when I panicked. But instead, I had to prove to Nolan that I could get over it.

Anger may have been the wrong motivation, but it was one that led me to possibly the stupidest decision of my life.

I grabbed the keys to his Maserati and stormed out of the office.

Chapter Twenty-Two: You Know What's Even More Frustrating Than Losing? When People Let Me Win

Nolan

After Blossom disappeared, I stared stubbornly at the screen of my laptop and clenched my teeth so hard that my jaw muscles ached.

Fuck. That had felt wrong. Not just bad, but seriously wrong, almost like we'd just ended our relationship.

Get a grip, Caldwell.

I hit the table with the flat of my palm, because anything else would have smashed my knuckles, and stood up. I needed a sparring session, and as luck would have it, my sparring partners were up on the roof, "secretly" smoking.

On my way up to the fire escape, I bumped into Karen, who rubbed at the black mark on her hand and smiled broadly when she saw that we were alone in the hallway.

"Wash that stain away, otherwise you'll ruin all my documents," I growled as I walked past.

"I've already tried three times," she called after me. As if her answer was an apology.

"Don't touch any paper in my company until your hands are clean." Then I disappeared through the fire door into the stairwell and ran up the stairs two steps at a time.

At the top, Dylan and Bruce turned around at the same time.

"Caught you," I said dryly.

"Congratulations, you've discovered our terribly kept secret," Dylan replied in the same tone.

"Which of you would like to spar?" I crossed my arms in front of my chest and tried not to let on how much I was boiling inside.

Blossom was gone. She had left me freezing in the rain, ripped my heart out of my chest, and thrown it on the floor in front of me. And why? Because I'd fucked someone else who meant nothing to me.

"You never fight outside the Haven." Dylan looked me up and down.

"The Haven is more practical," I replied.

"When I wanted to go to Hell's Kitchen to the fight club because it's convenient, you gave me a two-hour lecture on safety, sportsmanship, and other stuff that still makes my ears bleed today," he commented.

I remembered his offer, and the sermon I had given him, all too well.

"Why would a billionaire have to win money in illegal fights?" I asked, rubbing my throbbing temples. It was time to introduce my head to a few fists, so I could think clearly again.

"Because then it's about something. This is about nothing," he replied with a shrug. That was an argument, but only almost.

"It's about the fact that it needs to happen now." I undid my cufflinks, took off my jacket, and pushed my sleeves back. The fact that I was creasing my neatly pressed designer suit, even though I still had at least eight hours of work ahead of me, was a clear sign that I meant business.

"I still owe you an ass kicking, why not now?" Bruce put out his cigarette and took off his jacket. Unlike me, he made a point of not wrinkling his clothes.

"Okay, I'll just keep standing here and try to figure out what's got your panties in a twist," Dylan said, leaning against the wall.

"Shut up," I snapped, raising my arms to cover my face.

"Sure, buddy." His sarcastic tone made sure that we all understood that he didn't believe a word I said.

"Fuck you, Dylan." Then I looked at Bruce. "Ready?"

"Ready." He raised his hands in a fighting stance, then the exchange of blows began.

I had no patience for endless ducking and feinting today. I immediately went into full swing, and Bruce followed suit. The fists flew past my face, and my thoughts slowly calmed down a little.

"So it's completely normal for you two to fight on the roof of the company in your fine Bertani suits?" Dylan asked, lounging against the wall.

My response was nothing more than an annoyed growl as I continued to focus on Bruce. He faked to the left, then punched me in the stomach with his right fist. I briefly fell to my knees before forcing my body back into a fighting stance. The next blow struck my shoulder, then my chin. But instead of stopping, I kept pushing through.

This was exactly what I needed. Pain that distracted me. If there was one thing I had learned in my past, it was how to channel my pain and turn it into something useful. And that's exactly what I wanted now. Pain, so that I could focus my thoughts away from Blossom.

"What's going on?" I asked when Bruce stopped throwing punches.

"Do you know what's even more frustrating than losing to you?" he asked, frowning.

"No, but you're about to tell us," I replied, still hoping for a fight.

"If you let me win." He lowered his fists completely and stepped away.

"I'm not letting you win shit," I grumbled, feeling my fingers over the swollen part of my cheek.

"You may be able to lie to yourself, but you can't lie to us. We've known you for years. We're family, remember?" Dylan looked at me with a mixture of sternness and concern. "What happened, buddy?"

"Blossom rejected my request." Saying it was harder than I thought, because it made the defeat seem real. Maybe I had been nothing more than a contract to her after all, and accepting that fact was going to be damn hard if it was true.

"You proposed to her?" Dylan almost dropped the fresh cigarette he had been trying to light. "How the hell did that happen?"

"We had a fight. Then I proposed to her. And she refused." Saying it again didn't make it any better; on the contrary, it made me want to have this whole damn day beaten out of my head.

"More details," Bruce demanded. They both looked at me as if I'd lost my mind.

"There's nothing more to say," I grumbled sullenly.

"Shit, you propose to the first woman you've ever shown anything resembling feelings to, she turns you down, and you have nothing to say about it?" Dylan rubbed his temples. "What were you arguing about?"

I was half-tempted to grab a cigarette, but managed to stop myself at the last moment. If I betrayed my principles now, I would be completely lost.

"We had a fight about Karen. The usual jealousy drama." I still didn't understand why Blossom had reacted so sensitively, even though my position and intentions were clear.

"Any woman would go crazy when confronted with Karen. Need I remind you that you dumped her on me?" Dylan grimaced like he'd bitten into a lemon.

"No, you don't have to. But that should prove even more that I'm not interested in her," I pointed out. In my eyes, my behavior had been both logical and understandable.

"Rationally, yes, but emotionally it's hard to understand," said Dylan, tapping his index finger on his chest where his heart was.

"But there's nothing wrong with a no, I don't want to marry you." I spat out the words as if they were bitter as bile. Had I misinterpreted the way she looked at me? The warmth in her eyes when I pulled her close? Fuck. I didn't know anything anymore.

"Did you get down on your knees in front of her? Ring, magic moment and all?" Dylan asked, bringing me out of my thoughts.

"Since when have you been a romantic?" I countered with a frown.

"I'm not, but you should have at least Googled 'proposals' beforehand, otherwise you wouldn't have been so stupid as to throw a loveless proposal at Blossom's feet in an argument. No wonder she stormed off." He took one last drag before throwing the half-finished cigarette on the floor and walking away.

"A request is a request," I replied coolly.

"I hate to admit it, but I have to agree with Dylan. You fucked up, buddy, because a proposal isn't just a proposal," Bruce said.

I thought about it for a moment, and came to the conclusion that they were right. We had never talked about getting married, but when I thought about it, she had given hints and signs. She left romance novels lying around, and every time she watched a chick flick on TV, she got all sentimental.

"Guys, I fucked up." A sigh escaped my throat. "Now what?"

"Two choices." Dylan turned and raised two fingers in the air. "One, you don't get over your pride, you remain stubborn, and you forever regret not chasing after her. Or two, you apologize to her, and hope she doesn't hold it against you. And the next time you propose to her, don't do it in a fight. Or without a flash mob dancing a choreography to 'Can't Take My Eyes Off Of You' that would make them jealous on Broadway."

The answer was obvious, but I still had to think about it for a second. Not because I wasn't sure that she was my woman for life, but rather because I wasn't sure if I was the right man for her. But was it up to me to decide?

Blossom had always insisted on making her own decisions, so I couldn't patronize her now.

"You're right, I have to apologize. And then we'll throw Karen out."

Dylan threw his arms to the sky. "Good God, he's finally come to his senses!"

I patted him on the shoulder. "Thank you." Then I did the same to Bruce. "Thank you too. Also for not smashing my face in when you had the chance."

"Next time. Promise." He grinned wryly at me. "Now stop wasting your time and go get the girl back."

I stormed down the fire escape, back to my office, then took my phone out of the drawer and dialed her number. Silence. Then the voicemail came on.

"Hey boss." Out of the corner of my eye, I saw Karen peering curiously through the door.

"I'm not your boss anymore." I hadn't forgotten my plan to fire her, but there were more important things to sort out first.

I couldn't lose Blossom under any circumstances. I needed her in my life. Hell, she was my life.

"Is now a bad time to ask if we're going to Mercer Solutions in your Maserati?" she asked, tactless as always, because she had no sense of when I was busy.

"Your timing has never been worse." My eyes wandered across the table. "Where are the keys?"

"I don't know." She shrugged and I inhaled sharply as I realized what had happened.

Fuck, fuck, fuck.

I dialed Blossom's number again as I paced back and forth trying to find a solution to this problem. I had been too hard on her and I regretted every single word I had said. But most of all, I regretted not having the ability to confess the feelings I had for her.

"What is it?" Karen asked, unconcerned.

"Blossom took the car," I blurted, and that fact was like a punch in the stomach.

"I thought she didn't drive?" Her barbed tone provoked me to give her a heated glare.

"Obviously she does now. If she has an accident now..." My voice broke.

"Oh come on, the car probably won't go two blocks." She waved it off casually. But the certainty in her voice made me sit up and take notice.

"What makes you so sure?" Karen wasn't empathetic, nor did she believe in the best in people. So why did she suspect that the car would barely make it out of the garage?

"Um. Intuition?" She blinked at me and smiled away something that looked like guilt.

"Karen."

She continued to avoid my stern gaze, despite my sharp tone. I had no fucking patience for this.

"Get out of my office," I snapped at her, trying to concentrate on the facts at hand. I had to get Blossom back, no matter what. I needed her, dammit. I couldn't breathe without her. Reflexively, I loosened my tie and kept calling her number.

What could I say to her? There were a thousand things I had never said. And I was ready to say them all. Every single word, when she came back to me.

But the most important thing was that she got out of my car before she did anything stupid. If she had an accident now she would never forgive me, and there was no question that I would never be able to forgive myself either.

Our argument had forced her to act hastily, which I didn't blame her for. I had been a fucking idiot, and she had cut her teeth on me. In her eyes, this was her last chance to prove to me that she was right and that I had feelings for her. She had hit the bull's eye with her assumption.

I dialed her number again and again, hoping that she would answer before anything bad happened. Just the thought that maybe the worst had already happened almost killed me.

Come on, Blossom. Answer the phone!

Chapter Twenty-Three: Nolan, I Love You

Blossom

When I got into the car, I was still so angry that the fear didn't stand a chance. Not even when I adjusted the seat and the mirrors, realizing as I did just how tall Nolan actually was.

My hand slipped over the seatbelt, but I couldn't bring myself to buckle up, even when I saw Nolan's serious look in my mind's eye. Maybe I didn't fasten my seatbelt because I wanted to provoke him, to show him how little power he had over me.

But who was I kidding? It was only because of him that I had overcome my greatest fear. He had control over my heart, and therefore over my entire life.

I started the car and put it into first gear. Luckily for me, my dad had driven an ancient car, so the manual transmission was no problem for me.

What made me sweat more was the built-in navigation device. It took me five minutes to enter the destination address, after rummaging through dozens of other functions.

"Good God, you don't need a driver's license for this thing, you need a doctorate," I muttered, shaking my head after I'd finally figured it out.

I slowly eased the car out of its parking space and maneuvered it through the underground lot. It jolted a little for the first few yards, but then purred like a contented kitten until I reached the barrier that led outside. Because everyone here, including the security guards, was familiar with Nolan's fancy wheels, I was able to pass through the barrier without any problems.

My hands were clammy and I wiped them on my blouse, but soon I was merging into traffic, and within minutes the congestion in the streets eased as I left the city center behind me.

My heart was beating wildly, but I didn't give the fear any room. I was still far too angry with Nolan for that. When would that jerk finally realize how much he meant to me?

"Finally get over it." His words had cut so deep that I wondered if it could ever heal.

Two more miles until I reached my destination. Child's play.

Then a call lit up on my phone. It was him.

I hesitated briefly, but decided not to take his call. I was still too angry. He probably just wanted to make sure I didn't damage the paintwork again. The car gave a little shudder once in a while, which I put down to the fact that it had been a long time since I'd last driven a car with gears, or any car for that matter.

Just under a mile and a half to Florida Road. It wasn't the right Florida Road, but it represented something I should have been fighting long ago.

A quiet voice in the back of my head whispered to me that I had only made it this far because Nolan had helped me. And not because he drove me up the wall, but because he had spent every single one of his lunch breaks with me.

No one had ever done that for me before, and I doubted that I would ever meet another man who was prepared to do something similar for me.

The further I drove, the more the fear subsided, but the angrier I got at Nolan and the fact that sometimes he was the perfect man and then other times he was so... typical.

I'd genuinely thought I was something special for him. And then? Then Karen came along and rubbed it in my face that he'd been fucking her—without a contract, mind you—and shattered my illusion that he and I had a connection that was unique.

The only thing that was unique seemed to be my endless naivety.

Nolan called again, and this time I was tempted to take the call. But I couldn't bring myself to do it, and so it went to voicemail yet again.

Then I took a deep breath as I reached the road that had been giving me nightmares for years. Florida Road in New York looked very different to the one in Seattle. Here, the road connected two parts of the city over a serpentine hill, linked by a bridge that I could see from afar.

But just because the road looked different didn't make it any less threatening.

Come on, Blossom. You can do it.

It wasn't my voice I heard in my head, but Nolan's, which made my heart tighten painfully.

What was I even doing here? To be honest, I didn't know what I was hoping to achieve with this car ride, I just knew that it felt right to finally do it.

Nolan called again, and this time my phone had somehow synced with the bluetooth in his car, so the call came through the hands-free speaker system of the Maserati.

"Blossom!"

I jumped half a foot. He sounded angry. Not just angry, he was so sour-milk sour that it left me speechless. So much concentrated anger gave my heart such a painful stab that I couldn't breathe.

"Stop the car!" he ordered in a firm voice. His commanding tone reminded me of the many sleepless nights we'd had. And normally I was happy to obey his orders, but not this time.

"No," I replied curtly. "Not until I've proved to you that I'm serious."

And because the situation wasn't dramatic enough, it suddenly started to rain buckets. That was great. Everything bad had come together today, and I hoped that my negative karma would soon be used up. I just couldn't take any more bad news.

"That's not important, let me explain everything to you as soon as you've pulled the car over and just listen to me..." he began, but I didn't let him get a word in edgewise. I had a lot on my mind that needed to get out before I burst.

"No, you listen to me. I love you, Nolan. And I don't know what else I have to do to prove it to you. But whatever proof you need..." I paused and listened to my heart. "I'll give it to you."

The car started to jerk, but I put it down to the incline and the bad weather.

"Shit, you don't have to prove anything to me. Stop the car!" he shouted.

"Yes, I do. Because I don't know how else I can get you to show me that you love me too. I can feel that you do, but I can't see it. And I don't know how much longer I can stand not being able to see it. I don't know why a simple 'I love you' is so hard, but I hope that one day I'll be worth the effort of saying it." I sighed and tried to suppress the pain that was stabbing at my heart with a knife.

"Blossom! Stop the car!" I'd never heard him in such a rage before, and part of me hoped he was losing his cool because he was worried about me. But another, more rational part of me figured that he was just worried about the stupid car.

"First I have to achieve my goal," I replied seriously. He had challenged me to do this, and I had accepted the challenge. It was hard, and every fiber in my body wanted to jump out of the car immediately, but I fought it because it was the only way to conquer my fear. And once I had conquered my fear, there would be no more excuses for Nolan; he would have to follow suit and show me that he took our relationship just as seriously as I did.

"Are you wearing your seatbelt?" he asked when he realized that I had no intention of stopping the vehicle.

"Yes."

He heard through my lie immediately. "Buckle up. Right. Now." He took a deep breath. "And stop the goddamn car!"

I rolled my eyes; he sounded like a broken record. But something in his voice made me feel uneasy, so I sighed and buckled up, even though the seatbelt was almost cutting off my air.

"Nolan, how can I make you believe that I love you?" The car jerked harder and harder, and when I tapped the brakes to adjust speed for the next turn, nothing happened.

"Uh oh." Panic crept up inside me, which I tried to swallow. I slammed on the brakes but nothing happened. Fear gripped my stomach with ice-cold hands and squeezed tightly. The scars on my arm began to throb and the gnawing sound of scraping metal echoed in my head.

"Blossom! Talk to me! Stop the car, dammit!" He must have understood that something was wrong because he yelled even louder.

"I can't," I said quietly. My voice was shaking as violently as the rest of my body.

I frantically took my foot off the brake, pushed the pedal down again, and hoped that it would work at some point. But nothing happened as the next bend drew closer and closer and closer and I could do nothing but stare disaster in the face.

The car was going too fast. My life flashed before my eyes.

There was only one thing left to say.

"Nolan, I love you."

Chapter Twenty-Four: I Love You Too, Blossom

Nolan

Her voice echoed in my head forever, while at the same moment time stood still. A cruel feeling that got worse with every passing second.

I hated feeling as helpless as I did just then, and I hated even more that I couldn't do anything to change the situation.

"Nolan, I love you."

It was a simple sentence, but it resonated so much that my mind was racing. I couldn't breathe; my chest tightened so much that I could practically hear my ribs cracking.

Fuck!

So much sincerity, so much honesty was overwhelming, especially because it felt like they were her last, deliberately chosen words as she raced toward her demise. She could have told me anything. That she hated me because we'd argued, or that I'd fucked up. But instead she'd said that she loved me, and that made the situation even crueler for me.

"I love you too, Blossom," I replied breathlessly.

A clicking sound echoed in my ear. Silence followed.

Silence that made me furious and stunned at the same time, silence that froze time while my thoughts raced, silence that possibly heralded the worst thing that could have happened.

"Blossom, say something!" Deafening silence. "Blossom!" Nothing.

I had finally managed to say those words, and then...

Stop! I wasn't allowed to finish that thought or I would go completely crazy.

And I couldn't lose control now, I had to stay calm and keep a cool head, anything else wouldn't help.

There was no question that she had had an accident. If that was the case, emergency services would already be on their way. It was a feature that I had installed, and I was more than grateful for taking the manufacturer's advice today.

Karen, who was standing outside my office and noticed my panic, stuck her head through the door again. Today she showed a particularly great talent for being annoying.

"Are you all right?"

"Nothing's wrong!" I ran my hand through my hair, then rubbed my throbbing temples, which felt like they were going to explode. "Blossom had an accident."

"Oh no." She turned pale. Unusual, when she had as much empathy as a stone. "I didn't mean to."

"What?" I looked at her questioningly, then my eyes wandered down to her hands, which were still smeared with oil. Then I put two and two together. "Shit, what have you done?"

"Okay, I admit it. I may have disconnected a few wires." Her eyes were huge. "And believe me, crawling under your lowered car in these shoes was almost a miracle. If you knew how sturdy those hoses and cables are, you'd appreciate my effort and..."

"Why the hell are you sabotaging my car?" I wanted to shake her. I'd never been this angry in my entire life. Not even when my father had beaten me to the point of hospitalization. Even when my mom had left me with him, I hadn't been nearly as angry as I was right now.

"I thought if the car broke down, we'd have more time together so I could convince you that I'm the one for you." She smiled at me, not even beginning to realize the implications of her stupidity.

I was on the verge of reducing my entire company to rubble. "You obviously weren't thinking at all! But that's your style, isn't it? You never think of others."

"Hey, like you're known as a great humanitarian," she snapped back. Then something must have dawned on her, maybe as she realized that "we" would never be anything more than a figment of her imagination.

"What exactly did you cut?" I asked, trying to evaluate the extent of the damage as I continued to rapid-dial Blossom's phone over and over.

"I don't know, I'm a personal assistant, not a mechanic! Just some cables that looked unimportant. Some were dripping yellow liquid, others I didn't get at all." She shrugged and I couldn't help but bump into her as I left my office.

"Pray that nothing happens to her," I said icily. "You're fired. Get out of here!"

It took a second, then she realized it was over, and tears ran down her face in torrents, which I didn't give a damn about. All that mattered right now was Blossom's safety.

Dylan and Bruce were in the corridor, heading my way. Perfect timing.

"Blossom had an accident, we have to go!"

In the elevator, I brought them both up to speed. Neither of them could even begin to find the right words; they had both swallowed their tongues.

"Do you know where to find them?" Dylan finally asked. "Or do you need the GPS?"

"I know exactly where we have to go. To Florida Road." Where else would she be going? It was the only conclusion that made sense to me.

"What's she doing there?" Dylan looked at me as if I'd lost my mind, but I knew she was there. Even without having to track my car.

"It's a long story. She wanted to make up for my mistakes."

She confronted her demons so I could do the same. I understood her reasons, and they were more logical than I would have liked. If she had managed to overcome her fears, I could do the same.

My stomach tightened painfully, and for the first time in a long, long time I prayed to anyone who would listen that she would be safe.

I love you, Blossom. I love you more than should be possible.

Chapter Twenty-Five: No Fears. No Karens. No Doors

Blossom

I gripped the steering wheel tightly as I watched raindrops run down the shattered windshield. My legs were so heavy that I couldn't move them, and the rest of my body didn't work either.

It took me a while to process what had just happened. The car had flipped over, after I crashed into the road barrier, and the shock was so deep that I couldn't breathe.

Streptopelia turtur. Columba livia. Streptopelia decaocto.

Who would have thought that I would find myself in the same situation a second time?

Wait, no. The wrecked cars were the same, but Seattle and right now were worlds apart. Back then, there had been a college idiot at the wheel who had wanted to get into my best friend's panties, and had therefore overestimated himself.

Today, I drove myself into disaster because I had been determined to prove something to Nolan. If he found out what I had done to his car, he would hate me forever, that much was certain.

And when the fear spread that I might lose him, the accident suddenly became the least of my problems.

I stared stubbornly at the hood and checked whether the engine was going to catch fire. A small part of me expected it to start smoking any second, just like back then, but nothing happened.

The car was still and silent, only the tapping of the raindrops cut through the silence, which almost drove me mad.

I still didn't move an inch, but just looked down at the seatbelt over my chest that had saved my life. Nolan had saved my life. Without his words, I wouldn't have been able to bring myself to do it.

A sob escaped my throat, because I had damaged his car again. This time it wasn't just a bit of paint. His Maserati was probably totaled, and it was my fault.

That was it. I made peace inside that this accident was the death blow to our relationship, and emotionally prepared myself for moving back to Seattle after crawling out of the wreckage of the car. When my stupid body would finally snap out of its state of shock.

But no matter how far I ran, even if I made it to the end of the world, it would never be far enough to escape the feelings I had for Nolan. When I'd thought it was over, it wasn't my life that had passed me by, it was just the time I had spent with him.

It sounded a bit naïve, and definitely pretty stupid, but if I had the chance to turn back time, I wouldn't do it. I had always known that my time with Nolan would end in a broken heart, but I also had him to thank for the happiest time of my life. Which was exactly why I wouldn't have done anything differently.

In the distance, I could hear sirens wailing as they came closer, but I paid them no mind. I preferred to hold on to the memories I had, and the tiny spark of hope that Nolan wouldn't hold it against me that I had smashed up his car.

"Blossom!" His voice echoed in my head. I started to cry because it sounded too real to ignore. I had wanted to prove to him that I loved him, but instead I'd crashed his car; I was unable to process it all properly.

"Blossom, are you okay?" His voice sounded so genuine that my heart beat a little faster.

I bit the inside of my cheek and cursed my subconscious. I probably had a concussion that was playing tricks on me. Painful pranks that stemmed from the deepest desire I had—Nolan.

It was only when he ripped open the driver's door that I realized he was real. Either that, or my head had been hit harder than I thought.

"What are you doing here?" I asked in surprise.

"Why do you think?" He grabbed my face with both hands and looked down at me. "Are you okay?"

"I think so." I took a deep breath as tears ran down my cheek. "But your car is wrecked. I'm so sorry…"

Nolan loved this car, which was now just a big lump of metal with a special paint job. I should never have driven it, then none of this would have happened. Karen had brought out the worst in me, and I was ashamed of it. Maybe it was best if I grabbed Little Miss Scratchy and just got out of New York, because I just wasn't cut out for this city.

If I was honest with myself, I had to admit that I never got very far. My apartment was a dump, and my job at the Royal Red didn't even begin to cover the bills I had to pay every month.

Then he put a finger to my lips. "I owe you an apology, little dove."

I bit my lips, unable to say anything. He felt responsible, which made me feel even more guilty. It wasn't his fault that I had lost control of the car.

"I love you, Blossom," he said.

I blinked at him in confusion. His sudden confession took my breath away. For so long, I had wanted him to say those exact words, but now they caused an ambivalent feeling that I couldn't describe.

"You don't have to say that now," I replied quietly. They were the nicest words ever, but I didn't know how much meaning they had for him, or if he just felt obliged to say it to make me feel a little better. I could only see the car from the inside, but if it looked half as bad on the outside, it must have been a bad accident.

"Yes, I should have said it long ago," he replied seriously. "I love you, and I hope you can forgive me one day."

I didn't know how to respond. My heart was screaming to forgive him, and part of my head was even claiming that he hadn't done anything wrong. But all the chaos inside me confused me so much that I felt dizzy; I didn't know what to say.

I couldn't get a word out until the paramedics arrived. Not even when they said that I needed to go to hospital so that I could be checked over better. I just shook my head, fighting back tears and rising panic when I thought about the trip to Medical South.

I don't know how Nolan managed it, but within a few minutes he had organized a helicopter to fly us across the city.

He held my hand the whole time, which I was grateful for because he showed me a closeness that had never been there before. Still, the whole time I had to wonder if he was only doing it because he thought I had almost killed myself in an accident because of our argument.

I kept quiet, and Nolan didn't say a word either. There were so many unspoken things between us. Love, hate, and everything in between. I had a lot to say, but because I didn't know where to start, I kept silent. My feelings for him were so strong that I would never get rid of them, that much was clear.

But I didn't know if I could stand the fact that there were women like Karen, who would throw themselves at him without restraint.

From the helipad, I was pushed through endless corridors that scared me. Nolan continued to hold my hand, but when we passed a door with a sign that read "RESTRICTED ACCESS", he was stopped.

"I belong with her," Nolan said, so seriously that it gave me goosebumps. I wanted nothing more than for him to mean those words, but I still worried that it was more about obligation or guilt.

"Are you married?" asked one of the two paramedics.

"No." He wanted to say something else, but he was interrupted.

"Then you have no business behind that door."

The door opened and Nolan's jaw tensed. "Blossom." His dark eyes pleaded with me to let him pass.

"I need to think," I replied. "I love you, but I don't know if what we have is made to last. Not when the world around us is so unforgiving."

They were the hardest words I had ever had to say, and my heart desperately wanted to beat me black and blue for speaking them. He was my grumpy Prince Charming, that much was certain. The only question was whether I was also his Cinderella.

Then I was pushed through the hospital door and my hand slipped out of Nolan's, leaving me feeling incomplete and cold.

I watched him fight the urge to enter the forbidden area with every fiber of his body, but he controlled himself. For me. Because he wanted to give me the time I needed to think things through.

"I swear to you, Blossom, I will prove you wrong. And when I've proved you wrong, nothing will separate us. No fears, no Karens, and no goddamn hospital doors!"

Chapter Twenty-Six: Do You Trust Me?

Blossom

Sighing, I slipped off the bed and gathered my stuff, which was lying in a plastic bag next to me.

"What are you doing?" Vince asked, hitting me with a fatherly stare.

"I'm getting dressed." I pulled my clothes out of the bag and countered his stern look. "Turn around."

"At least wait for the test results," said Ruby, standing in solidarity at Vince's side. Traitor.

"What are they supposed to tell me? I'm fine. No scratches, no whiplash. But there's a good chance I'll pass out and crack my head open when I get the bill."

"She's joking, that's a good sign, isn't it?" asked Ruby, looking in Vince's direction.

"That's not a valid diagnosis issued by a doctor," he pointed out.

The two were registered as my emergency contacts, and as it turned out the decision had been spot on. Both had dropped everything at the Royal Red when they got the call.

"Assuming they release you right this second, where are you going?" asked Vince.

"Home," I replied. Wherever home was. Probably not with Nolan anymore.

Oh God, Little Miss Scratchy was still with him! It tore my heart out, but I guess I had to leave her with him until I found a suitable home for us. I definitely didn't want her to have to sleep with me in some filthy motel.

"Anywhere. The main thing is to get out of here," I mumbled to myself. I hadn't had the heart to tell them about the fight between Nolan and me. Or that we'd been separated. The only constant in our relationship seemed to be not knowing where we were in our relationship.

I breathed out heavily when I thought of the chaos that awaited me out there. But the white walls and the backless hospital gown were choking me. I'd never been good at waiting.

Besides, I felt fine. At least physically. No broken bones, no internal bleeding. Apart from the broken heart, which couldn't be seen on an X-ray.

"Do you know why I took the stupid car in the first place?" I asked. Out of consideration for me, they hadn't asked about the accident yet, for which I was infinitely grateful.

"No. And you don't have to tell us, the main thing is that you're okay." Vince smiled mildly at me. "And because I really want you to be okay, I won't let you go until a doctor gives the okay."

He stood with his arms folded in front of the curtain that separated us from the corridor. A meaningless gesture, since the curtain was open on the other two sides, but I understood that he meant what he said.

Ruby sat down at the foot of the bed and took my hand. "Whatever happened, it wasn't your fault."

I pulled a face. "Yes, it was. I was angry enough to think I could conquer my fear. And then I wrapped Nolan's beloved car, which is something of a holy grail for him, around the nearest guardrail. Because I wanted to prove something to him. Something pretty stupid, to be precise." Shaking my head, I reviewed this morning in fast-forward. Sometimes I really was more naive than was good for me.

"To prove what?" Ruby asked curiously.

"That you can beat your fate if you're brave enough. But I seem to be cursed somehow." I wasn't joking, it really felt like destiny had it in for me.

"I think you're taking it pretty well," she replied dryly and patted me gently on the shoulder.

"Wait and see how much composure I have the next time I have to get into a car." I bit my lips as tears burned behind my eyelids. Last time, Nolan had helped me deal with my anxiety. Who would help me now?

Even though I was stuck in a hospital full of people with Ruby and Vince, I felt terribly lonely because I missed Nolan. He was the only one who had ever managed to break through my protective wall.

"We'll work it out somehow." Ruby patted my hand again. She wasn't good at this sort of thing, so I appreciated her trying all the more.

"Did you and Nolan have a fight?" Vince sat down at the head of the bed and gently pushed on my shoulder, forcing me to sit down as well.

"Fight isn't the right word. I think we broke up." It was infinitely painful to say it, but it had to come out.

Ruby's lips formed a wide "O" of astonishment. "I don't believe that. You two were like peanut butter and pickles. Kinda weird, but it totally worked."

"But we were also like cat and mouse." With a dull shrug, I let my legs dangle over the gray and white vinyl floor. "I'm sure he hates me because I wrecked his car." He hadn't driven it a single mile since it got back from Europe.

"But wasn't he the first one on the scene?" Vince looked at me, frowning. I don't know how he knew that. He had probably overheard it in some conversation with the nurses.

People were whispering about my accident all over the hospital, but especially about Nolan. His name was being murmured everywhere.

"Yes, he got me out of the car," I finally admitted.

"Did he tell you that he hates you?" Vince continued. He was normally a quiet guy, but this seemed to really upset him.

"No, on the contrary, he said that he loves me," I replied. He gave me a knowing look.

"Well, there's your answer." Ruby nodded her head vigorously in agreement.

"But he probably only said that because he felt obligated to. Because of my shock and things like that," I said. Who knew if what he'd said was really true, or just wishful thinking.

"Or maybe he said it because he really loves you. Plausible to me," Ruby countered.

"For me too," Vince agreed.

I let her words sink in for a few seconds. What if it was true?

No. I had to stay realistic, and not get my hopes up. The more I hoped for it, the more painful the fall that awaited me would be. And the highs with Nolan had been so high that the lows were unforgiving.

"Are you both conspiring against me today?" I asked, because I had nothing else to say to them.

"We only want the best for you. And the best is Nolan." Vince put his hand on my knee and I bit the inside of my cheeks to keep from crying, because any kind of physical closeness was overwhelming right now.

"I thought you hated him." I sniffled.

"I'm not his biggest fan, but he's good for you," Vince said, which honestly amazed me because it must have taken him a lot of effort to say it.

"Hear, hear. Vince has given his okay, which means the way to the registry office is clear," Ruby cheered, grinning wryly at me.

"He's proposed to me before," I muttered sullenly.

"You. Can't. Be. Serious." Her jaw fell practically to her knee as she stared at me with huge eyes.

"Yes, I am. That's how our argument started." I sighed theatrically to make it clear that there was no short version of the story, but I didn't want to go too far.

"Boy, oh boy. Everything is really coming together today." Ruby rubbed her forehead with her hand. "Did I miss anything else? An alien invasion? Leaks of Henry Cavill's secret phone that he only uses for nudes?"

"Why would Henry Cavill have a phone for nudes?" I asked.

"Everyone has a phone with photos like that on it," she said, with such conviction that I blinked at her. Vince and I exchanged meaningful glances, which Ruby ignored. "Anyway, if you hadn't just gone through a horrible crash..." I gave her an annoyed look, because her embellishments weren't making anything better, but she just ignored me. "... I would be shaking you up right now."

"Why?" I tilted my head and waited for an answer.

"Because Mr. Right proposed to you and you turned him down! Are you still okay? If I were you, I would have accepted the proposal. Not just with a yes, or a double yes, but with a triple yes!" She threw her bright red hair over her shoulder and the tips almost whipped my face.

"It's not that simple," I replied, holding my hand protectively in front of my face.

"Hey, I've never turned down a proposal before." She put her hands on her petite hips and turned her flushed cheeks away from Vince, who was suddenly listening very closely to our conversation.

"No, you just left someone at the altar," I countered.

Vince raised an eyebrow. Uh oh. Ruby obviously hadn't told him about the little Vegas incident.

"Oh God, that's no comparison!" She rolled her eyes.

"No?" I let the question hang there, knowing she'd take the bait, and she did.

"A night of drinking in Vegas that ends in front of an Elvis chapel is totally different from what you and Nolan have," she said heatedly, earning an interested look from Vince.

"Well, I guess the only thing he and I have left now is the custody battle over Little Miss Scratchy."

He had taken her to his heart and she loved to curl up on his chest when we were in bed. It wouldn't just be hard for me, that much was certain. My heart tightened when I thought about the fact that she was still in his apartment, and that it would have to stay that way until I had a new apartment.

There was no question about my little kitty living in a shabby motel until we found something less ragged that I could afford. If I could afford anything at all. In addition to the total loss of the Maserati—which, if I added up the cost of the special paint job, had cost me at least a billion dollars by now—there was also the hospital bill, which I was sure I would have to work my whole life to pay for.

"Since when have you been such a doomsayer?" Ruby asked, snapping me out of my thoughts.

"Ever since I realized I wasn't right for Nolan." I couldn't deny that he was my Mr. Right. He definitely was, but I wasn't the right woman for him, and there was nothing I could do about that.

"What makes you so sure?" She looked at me uncomprehendingly.

"I just can't bring myself to ignore all the Karens in this world who are systematically throwing themselves at him," I explained. It wasn't a good plan, but it was better than having no way of protecting my heart at all.

"Do you know what helps against Karens? Even the really nasty ones? An anti-chafing wedding ring. Which he's already offered you, mind you." She waved her hand in front of my face, emphasizing the ring finger.

"In the most unromantic way he could think of." I snorted. "During an argument where emotions were running high."

The worst part was that a piece of me had almost said yes, because I had never wanted anything else. I wanted to be his wife. Mrs. Nolan Caldwell.

Vince cleared his throat. "But that's what you wanted. For him to show emotion, which I think he obviously did."

The world really had to be upside down today if even Vince took sides with Nolan.

"Yes, but differently." I hated him for backing me into a corner that I couldn't talk my way out of. Why did the two of them have to come up with so many logical arguments, now of all times, to fuel my hopes of a happy ending? My life was not a fairy tale where everything would magically turn out well in the end.

"That can be arranged." It wasn't Ruby or Vince who had spoken, but Nolan, who pushed the curtain aside and stood in front of me in the flesh. "But first, there are other things to sort out."

Ruby slid off the bed and cleared her throat. "Um, I'm going to check out the cafeteria. They have donuts." When Vince didn't respond, she nudged him in the ribs with her elbow. "I bet you want some too, don't you?"

"Um." He looked at me questioningly, but I nodded at him, signaling that I was okay. "Sure."

They both disappeared, leaving us as much privacy as we could get when we were only separated from my fellow patients by a few cloth sheets on a metal rod.

"How long were you eavesdropping?" I asked. Heat shot into my cheeks; I didn't want him to know about my soul striptease with my friends.

"Not for long," he assured me. He looked me up and down, full of concern, but also relieved.

"And how did you even get in here?" I asked once I had got over the shock of his appearance.

He grinned lopsidedly at me. "You know me. When I want something, I get it."

"Of course. You bribed the security guard." I said what came into my head. But he shook his head.

"Almost." He placed his thumb and forefinger close together. "I bought the hospital."

I grinned, forgetting for a second the tragedy that was my life, but he remained serious. He wasn't joking. He had bought a hospital because of me. As always, he was incorrigible.

"Nolan, I know you're expecting an answer from me, but..."

"I don't expect anything, except for you to listen to me." He took my hand. "Today was a terrible day. That's why I want you to remember the good part when you think back on today. Not the bad things."

A nice thought, but unfortunately the bad events far outweighed it today and I couldn't think of anything that could make up for it.

"But nothing good has happened." I blew a strand of hair out of my face. "Unless you're saying that your lunchtime pastrami sandwich from Daisy's was so memorable that it makes me forget the car crash." I was joking, but I didn't feel like laughing at all. On the contrary, I wondered how I had managed not to cry so far.

"Their sandwiches are good, but not that good." He handed me a box that looked like the one I'd been given before the big gala.

"What's this?" I fiddled with the big red ribbon that the package was wrapped in.

"Open it," he demanded.

I opened the box and pulled out a red dress. My red dress. The one with the long sleeves that I loved so much, the deep neckline, and the slit up the side that showed off my long legs.

"Put it on." Nolan's tone almost forced me to obey him. But with the last of my strength, I managed to resist.

"I still have to wait for the test results," I replied. It was an excuse, but one that worked.

"The doctors say you're okay," he replied quickly, but with enough certainty for me to believe him.

"Of course you would know about that too." Even before I did. There was nothing Nolan Caldwell didn't seem to have control over.

"Do you think I was just going to wait out there until someone might tell me how you are? I couldn't just sit there and do nothing. So I made sure you were okay and now I'm going to make sure you never forget this day."

"Trust me, I will never forget this day."

"In a good way."

I didn't blame him, because I would have done the same in his place if our roles had been reversed. Or at least I would have tried with the three dollars I still had in my pocket.

"I don't know," I stammered uncertainly. I didn't know anything anymore. Neither where my head was, nor what my heart actually wanted.

"Do you trust me?" He scrutinized me with his dark eyes, and that convinced me.

"Yes." I nodded. Just because we'd had a terrible argument today hadn't changed my trust in him. Nolan hadn't given me a single reason to doubt that, so I couldn't doubt him now either.

"Then keep trusting me, little dove."

He held out his hand and looked at me expectantly. I should resist him, otherwise it would only be more painful to let go of him for good, but I was too weak. I took his hand.

"Okay."

Chapter Twenty-Seven: Ask Me Again

Nolan

I led Blossom outside, where a hybrid electric car was waiting for us. It was the safest model on the market, a fact which I explained to her in detail.

"Trust me," I said as I helped her get in and fastened her seatbelt for her. "There won't be another accident." My hands stayed on her body longer than was appropriate, but she didn't resist. Even now, even after the most horrible thing that could happen between us, there were still feelings that made the air around us crackle.

"How do you know that?" she asked after I closed her door and got behind the wheel.

"Because I had the roads closed until we reach our destination," I replied seriously.

"I'm not even going to ask how you did that." She looked at me, shaking her head, but a wry smile crept onto her lips.

"Let's just say a few people on Twenty-Third owe me one." Aside from a favor, everyone was understanding of the situation, and would have helped me even without an honor debt.

I started the car and drove off, but not fast enough for Blossom to tense up. Even if we only drove five miles an hour, I didn't care. The road would be closed off long enough.

"Are you okay?" I asked, watching her out of the corner of my eye.

"I'm fine," she said, her lips drawn into a thin line. "I'm not behind the wheel."

"Now that you mention it..." I had no idea how to tell her about Karen's sabotage. It would shake her worldview to its very depths, and I was afraid it would destroy something inside her.

"Yes?" She looked at me expectantly, forcing me to answer.

"The accident wasn't your fault, it was Karen's." I sighed, searching feverishly for better words, but I couldn't think of any. I wasn't usually at a loss for words, but for some reason I was completely tongue-tied.

"If you look at it from all angles, that could be true," she said with a shrug.

"She screwed around with the car." The answer wasn't pretty, or particularly emotive, and I hated myself for not being able to just speak what was on my mind.

As she processed my words, her eyes grew huge.

"Why? I thought she wanted to go to Mercer Solutions with you. Then why would she sabotage the car?"

I laughed bitterly, because I still couldn't believe what had actually happened.

"Her plan was for the car to break down so she could spend extra time with me."

"Seriously?" Now she was laughing. Not in a bitter or cynical way, she laughed out loud like I'd made a fucking joke.

"What's so funny about that?" I was confused, and wondered if she was in shock. It had to be shock, otherwise she wouldn't be behaving so strangely.

"She sabotaged the car to win you back, and instead it led to the exact opposite." She cleared her throat. "Sort of, at least."

"If you're saying we're rid of her, you're damn right we are, because my lawyers will make sure of it."

After I found out about Blossom, Bruce and Dylan had been able to implement the rest of my plan to sic every single one of my lawyers on Karen.

"You fired her?" She exhaled with relief and leaned back in her seat, looking a little more relaxed.

"I didn't just fire her, I'm going to make sure she goes to jail. It's the least I can do after what she did to you," I growled. My hands gripped the steering wheel, so tightly that my knuckles turned white. Even her name was a red flag for me from this day on, and would remain so for the rest of my life.

"You want her in prison?" Blossom looked at me questioningly. Was that pity on her face?

"Yes. She almost killed you. That's attempted manslaughter." I had expected her to be pleased to know that Karen would never stand in our way again, but she grimaced.

"Isn't that a bit harsh? She didn't know I was going to steal your car to prove something to you."

"She deserves it." I stuck to my decision. "If she hadn't sabotaged the car..."

"Believe me, reliving the accident was hard," she cut me off. "But it was also... good." She spoke slowly and carefully, and I might have believed her if I hadn't pulled her out of the wreckage of a totaled car a few hours ago.

"Good? Do you want me to take you back to the hospital?"

"I'm doing extremely well. In a metaphorical sense, or whatever you want to call it, in view of today's events." She looked at me seriously and I returned her gaze.

"Are you going to let her get away with it?"

"No, of course not. But she loved you, and she was desperate. I had the same knee-jerk reaction that she did when I took your car."

"That's completely different."

"Is it?"

"Okay, there is some overlap. But you didn't mean to hurt anyone. Not intentionally or unintentionally." I sighed. "I should have made it clear to her earlier that I didn't want anything from her."

"And I shouldn't have reacted so with so much jealousy; I should have believed you instead." She gave me a grin. "She even got her hands dirty for you. She won't be getting rid of those oil stains any time soon."

"I would have expected a lot of answers, but not like this."

"What then? Something biblical, like an eye for an eye, or should it be more poetic?" She shook her head. "You know what would be much worse for her than jail? If she had to do community service, because she never wants to do anything for anyone."

"Is that what you want?"

"Yes. At least it's a positive thing. Karen can help make the world a little better. Even if she won't care at all."

"What have I done to deserve you?" I asked, stunned. She had just survived a car accident that Karen had caused, and all she could think about was how she could help others. I don't know how many hours I'd spent thinking about throwing my father into some dark hole—if he'd still been alive—but it showed again that Blossom was a better person than me.

She took a deep breath to say something. The look she gave me was divine, and I would have killed to see it a second time. But we had reached our destination and she faltered when she realized that we were standing in the middle of the Metropolitan Opera House, with crowds of people pressing toward the entrance.

"What are we doing here?" She looked around for an answer.

"We're going to a concert. A fully booked concert, to be precise," I replied.

"Who's playing?" Her gaze lingered on a large poster directly above the entrance to the house and she swallowed hard as she saw herself. "This is a bad joke, isn't it?"

"No." I put on a serious face and gave her no reason to believe that it wasn't true.

"But I can't play." Reflexively, she rubbed her arm, which was scarred from her accident, and I put my hand on hers.

"You can, I've seen you play dozens of times." Blossom wasn't just playing, she was feeling the music she had written herself. It wasn't my money that had drawn people to the concert today, it was her talent.

"What if my hand cramps?" She stared at her hands as if they were old enemies.

"Every single person in the audience knows," I reassured them. Nevertheless, the venue was booked to the last seat, because nobody wanted to miss the chance to see a new star in the sky of talented musicians.

"And they still want to hear me?" she asked, blinking at me in surprise.

"Otherwise, they wouldn't be here to write reviews about you." With that, I dispelled her doubts. Or at least, I defused her nervousness enough for her to believe my words.

"You're incredible." She stared, open-mouthed, at the packed square and the dense crowd in front of us.

"No, you're incredible," I replied with a smile.

I helped her out of the car and led her into the Met via the side door, because she wasn't ready for the media frenzy outside the main entrance. Dylan met us there, and led us to the stage, where we stopped and stared at the packed house.

"Can you hear how hard my heart is beating?" Blossom asked. She took my hand and placed it on her chest. It literally jumped against her ribs.

"You'll charm her," I replied with a smile. I'd never cared much about music before, it was only when I'dmet her that I realized what music could do and change. My whole life, for example.

I took her hand and looked at her seriously. "There's also a substitute player if you don't feel up to it. I want you to play voluntarily because it's always been your dream. I want you to live your dream instead of feeling indebted to an audience you owe nothing to. Do you want to play?"

"I can't believe I'm saying this, but yes. I want to play."

"Good." I smiled. "Your sheet music is ready, I had it all brought in from the Royal Red." As if they had heard our conversation, Ruby and Vince waved to us, who also had a seat in the front row.

"I'm ready." Blossom nodded resolutely, then went on stage and after a brief round of applause, she began to play.

She always played well, but today she outdid herself. I got goosebumps after the first few notes, and when I looked at Bruce and Dylan, who knew as little about music as I did, I could see that they felt the same way. The rest of the audience also sat back and relaxed, enjoying the atmosphere that had settled over the room.

Blossom was made for the big stage, that much was certain. And now that I saw how she shone, I wanted to drag her onto every big stage in the world.

Today, Blossom had not only overcome her fears, but also realized her biggest dream. Whether she wanted me back or not, I was happy because I had made her world a little better.

"She's incredible," whispered Dylan as the last notes echoed through the concert hall.

"She is," I agreed with him. Just then I was even prouder of the fact that she was my little dove, if that's what she still wanted to be. She was wearing my necklace and that had to mean something, right?

As the rapturous applause slowly died down, she waved me over, begging with her eyes until I joined her on stage.

"Ask me again," she whispered breathlessly. Her whole body shook with excitement and tears of joy made her emerald eyes shine even brighter.

I looked at her questioningly.

"Ask me again if I want to marry you," she demanded, still breathing heavily with excitement.

"Now?" There was no way I was going to steal the show. It was her big moment, not mine.

"When else? Or are you not prepared?" Blossom teased, grinning wryly at me.

I grinned back in victory, then pulled a small velvet box out of my trouser pocket and got down on my knees in front of her.

"Blossom Rush, love of my life, will you marry me?" I opened the box and out came a silver ring. Instead of a diamond, a small flying dove adorned the top.

"Nolan Caldwell, love of my life, yes, I want to marry you," she replied and held out her hand to me, trembling with excitement.

Our first kiss as fiancés was accompanied by another round of applause, which I completely ignored. All that mattered just then was that we were together and would stay together. Forever.

"I love you, Blossom."

"And I love you, Nolan."

Acknowledgments

A thousand thanks to my hard-working test readers, my dear colleagues and my husband, without whom there would be no novels from me. And a thousand thanks to you for reading this book. I am open to your criticism and praise, because I am a real person with real feelings. You can always write to me at lanaherself@lana-stone.com.

There are no contraceptives in this book, why? It's not set in the real world, but in the Lanaverse, where not only do all the billionaires have six-packs and are good in bed, but there are also no sexually transmitted diseases or unwanted pregnancies. It's a dream world where you can just let yourself drift and forget about reality.

If you would like to receive a free novel and be alerted when my next book is published, visit: https://lana-stone.com/. There, like over 9000 fans before you, you can sign up for my newsletter.

Printed in Great Britain
by Amazon